Build Me Up, Buttercup

By: James McDunn

Chapter 1
"Danny"

Mondays in the investment brokerage business are all pretty much the same. Actually, every day in the investment brokerage business *is* the same. I start by studying the market, seeing what is going up, and what is going down and call people and tell them about it. The more excited I can get about it, the more excited I could get them about it. The more excited I get about it equates to more sales. When you are one of the richest and most successful brokers on Wall Street, you are mighty good at getting that excited.

If I wasn't calling someone, someone was calling me. When I call, it is usually good, or at least I was trying to convince them it is good. When they call me, it is usually bad. It usually means that something I sold them was tanking and they were calling to yell at me because it was.

I stared at the computer screen and watched a million numbers go up and down and tried to remember which ones were going in what direction. It sort of reminded me of music on the page, which is what studied in college. If had a piano here, I could probably play it, but it wouldn't sound like anything anyway. But if I did that instead of this, I wouldn't be making nearly as much money as I am now.

This time, the phone ringing actually jarred me out of converting the NASDAQ into Beethoven. As I completed the most recent conversion from dollars to Euros, I listened for the rings. After the second one, I still wasn't done but I picked up the phone anyway:

"Danny Cullen", I answered. It was Ward Jenkins, one of my larger clients. He was also one of my most loquacious one, as well. His calls were always filled with plenty of opportunity to contemplate my life, as I pretended to listen. As he screamed and bellowed about how he wasn't getting the performance he wanted out of his seven-figure portfolio, my eyes wandered over to the name tag on my desk: "D. P. Cullen" was written in big brass letters. Above it, on the wall were newspaper clippings in frames of how I closed more business faster than anyone ever had on Wall Street.

"Hmm", I thought to myself. "I certainly look tall standing next to the Governor of New York. …but I need a hair cut". I am a little bit taller than most men; six foot two. My blondish, curly hair covers my ears and flops over my collar in this picture. My goofy Irish smile, I think, makes me look kind of stupid.

As I sit here, with my feet on the desk, pondering my life as an investment planner, and my subsequent success, I am taken by one fact: I am not really this guy. I am not Daniel Philip Cullen, at least I wasn't always. My real name, at least the one that I was born with, is not that much different. I was born Daniel Patrick McCullen, the son of a tool and die maker from Altoona, Pennsylvania. When you went to some little Community College in "nowheres-ville" PA, and finished somewhere near the middle of your class from the public university, doors don't automatically spring open. Middle Class Irishmen like me may have been the norm in coal mining towns like Altoona, but in big cities, where the money is, we are treated like second-class citizens. To make matters worse, having an Irish last name can turn you into a third class citizen before potential employers ever look at your resume. The glass ceiling certainly existed, not only from the Anglo-Saxons who put us there, but even from us blue-collar Irish who found it and obeyed it. Us Irish were told by other Irishmen that we were supposed to go to high school or into the Army, get out, go back to the mine or the factory where our fathers worked and where we worked every summer from 16 years old on, drink a 6-pack of cheap beer every night and die young and fat. In between, we were supposed to find a little, fat wife, pound out six or seven kids, send them to Catholic school, go to church on Sunday and be drunk shortly after 9:45 mass.

It might have been the blueprint for many young, dumb Catholic young men. Oh, I will grant you I was young and as dumb as all of the rest of them and as Catholic as the Pope, but I resented how they, the upper crust treated me and even how they, the blue-collar, potato-eating Mick-Irish treated me, as well. Money would be nice, and everything, I would take some if there were passing it out, but being treated like I was a dumb immigrant gnawed in my craw.

After two failed attempts at Music School, I finally graduated with a C- average. There are not a lot of things you can do with a degree in music if you are a mediocre musician. I found myself doing the only thing I seemed suited for. I got a job in a record store in one of the dumpier corners of New York City selling vintage record albums. We had the market cornered on the music of the Ars Nova *and* the Ars Antigua periods. Before you get any big ideas, I should tell you that having *that* market cornered is not that hard to do.

That previous life was never going to make the Society Page, or anything. I had Wednesdays off and worked three nights a week and all day Saturday and Sunday. That may seem like a drag to some people, but there was nothing much happening during those times that I would be interested in doing anyway. My apartment was lavishly furnished with a bean-bag chair, a black and white television, which I never turned on unless Notre Dame was playing football and a stereo on cinder blocks and long wooden planks. In the bedroom there was a mattress. There was some other stuff in the kitchen, like a dishwasher and a stove, but I never used them. I had no idea what to do with the stove, but the refrigerator did keep my beer cold.

One day, When the God of mediocrity turned His back, my destiny changed. Someone left a copy of Fortune Magazine on the counter of the record store. Since I had already read the liner notes of every Gasparo Alberti album 5 times, I decided to read it during my break. That was the day I made the shocking discovery: it was not that much harder to be rich than it was to be poor. The key was in Investment Planning. Being an Investment Planner, selling stocks and bonds, was not only lucrative but didn't require "rocket-science" intelligence. All it required was lots and lots of hours on the job. The beauty is, people have to pay me whether they wanted to buy stocks or to sell them. All I had to do was smear a load of horse hockey onto the latest thing I was trying to sell and then watch the fish line up, just waiting for me to slide the hook into their jaws. I decided, then and there, to change my life and to become an investment planner. Maybe I did it because I was bored. Maybe I did it to prove that I wasn't some stupid Irish kid from Altoona Pennsylvania. Despite the reason why I did it, I did it. I decided it was time, once and for all, to break the glass ceiling.

Since I was going to sell my soul to the Devil, I decided I should do it at the most heartless financial institution in North America. Fortunately for me, the investment firm of Gifford, Larkin and Glen had a training program, complete with a training salary that was slightly more than what the record store was paying for the first 90 days. After that, all I had to do put food on the table (which I didn't own) was to have no heart, disconnect my brain, and tell a hundred people a day that whatever product that I was placing before them was the next Microsoft. It was like shooting fish in a barrel. All I had to do was to do it. And do it I did. Before long, I had made as much each month and I was used to making in a year.

Part of that "soul selling" arrangement would require a few changes in my life – I would have to stop being an Irish Catholic Democrat and become an Anglo-Saxon Protestant Republican. The upper crust likes their own. Just like they wouldn't buy stock from someone named Goldberg, they wouldn't buy it from someone named McCullen. So, after some paperwork, 6 strategically placed ads in the most obscure newspapers in the world and two hundred dollars, Daniel Patrick McCullen became Daniel Philip Cullen.

Dropping the "Mc" from my last name made me sound less like an immigrant and more like a blue blood. Some people that I worked with actually took to calling me "Phil". When I asked someone why they did that, they said, "well, your father was Daniel, wasn't he?" They had no idea that my father worked in a coal mine in Altoona, Pennsylvania and that his first name was really Aloysius. I learned in the years to come that if you are part of that world, all men, from father to son, grandfather to grandson, had the same first name. If you didn't get labeled as a "Chip" or a "Flip" or a "Buddy", you were differentiated from your father by being addressed by your middle name. That simple rule of social etiquette made me glad that I left off the other L and spelled it "Philip". It made me sound more snooty.

Now, all I had to do was divest myself from everyone from my previous life and acquire a whole new cadre of friends and compatriots in the new one. After all, I couldn't have some Drunken Irish Hooligan flap up next to me at the Millionaire's Club Breakfast singing "Toorah, Loorah, Loorah" now could I?

That last bit of career planning was not that hard, since I didn't have that many friends in the first place. The stray bar-buddy barely knew that I was gone. My one and only girlfriend, Gloria Jean, the Jelly Bean, as I grew to call her, got messed up on hard drugs and disappeared into a pretty shady life. She was good at finding me, however, whenever she needed money, which was the only reason she looked for me at all. I would always give it to her, partially because I didn't need her as evidence of a previous life, and partially out of the guilt of having given her three hundred dollars six years ago, along with a phonebook opened to the listings of abortion clinics. She said that the baby was mine. I didn't really have the time or the wherewithal to debate it with her. I was in the midsts of my big career catharsis.

There were a few things that I would miss about her. When I wasn't calling her "Jelly Bean", I took to calling her "Murgatroid". That stemmed from when we were going to a Halloween party, and she insisted that we dress up as Raggedy Ann and Andy. I was late picking her up and when I got to her door, she hurriedly opened the door to reveal her thick red hair that was curled as tight as turnips. She did that to look more like her character, but not being used to seeing her like that, I said the first thing that came to my mind, which was a poem my crazy Irish grandmother used to say, "Mother Mary Murgatroid, who curled your hair so tight?" At first, she just stared at me, but within a few seconds she burst into laughter. She laughed so hard that I started to laugh at her laughing. Before we knew it, we were both laughing so hard that we were crying – which led to kissing – which led to…well, let me put it this way, we never made it to the party. That incident was probably the reason we needed the abortion clinic in the first place.

Things in my new life were skyrocketing. Every month, I finished in the top five, sales-wise at GLG, as they referred to themselves as. It was not that uncommon to finish in the top three. Occasionally, I would finish number one. My efforts were rewarded by 24 gold karat GLG cufflinks, expensive pens and wristwatches and other contest prizes plus barrels and barrels of money. My routine was set: be in the office at 7:00 AM, call people until 11:30 or 12:00, have an expensive power-lunch, always with some rich capitalist whose money I was trying to pry away, back at the office by 2:00, to be followed up by more phone calls until 4:30 or 5:00, when I would repeat the process over a power-dinner and a wealthy benefactor, then back to the office for even more phone calls until 8:30 or 9:00, then home, to 3 shots of Jameson's and into bed. That happened six days a week. Sundays were reserved for golf in the summer and skiing in the winter, again always with some client who had more money than common sense and the vast desire to give it to me. Don't get me wrong, it wasn't like I was holding these clients up at gunpoint or anything. I made them money; lots of money, but it wasn't anything they couldn't do by simply reading the Wall Street Journal and following the trends. But they didn't have time for that. They paid me to do that for them. And do that I did, while I was taking their money.

One of the rewards for my selling my soul to the devil was a 5 bedroom townhouse in one of the most expensive buildings in the upper east end of Manhattan. I had a decorator furnish the place, since I couldn't tell a davenport from an armoire in the first place. It didn't make any difference to me what they put in there, because I spent very little time in the townhouse anyway. I worked in my office and slept in my bed. Sometimes, I slept on the couch in my office.

The rules for my success were to always know exactly how much money to extract from each client and to always answer my phone and cell phone by the second ring. As long as I could follow those two rules, I could keep up the guise that I was one of "us" and not one of "them". I was too busy to be lonely, always chasing the next big deal. Thinking about it in retrospect, maybe that was the point in the first place. If I was busy making money, I didn't have to think about, or worry about being so lonely. Before I knew it, five years had gone by and I was on the verge of being a millionaire.

Chapter Two
"Gloria Jean"

There were a million things wrong with my life, but none the least of these was the fact that I was addicted to heroin. This was closely followed up by the fact that I had no visible means of support, was homeless and had a five-year-old daughter in tow. My ex-boyfriend's grandmother used to say, "God must love poor people, because He sure made plenty of them". If that were true, God surely loved me. It wasn't as though I didn't know how any of this happened to me. I was always a shy, lonely kid who never felt like she fit in. It seemed as though life was a class in college that I missed the first day of, when the teacher divulged the secrets for passing. Everyone else understood the rules of engagement, which they followed with pin-point precision, while I jutted and stalled and stammered through every social situation that was presented to me. It could have had something to do with the fact that my father killed himself, by placing a hose in the gas-pipe of his car and proceeded to go to sleep in it. I do remember walking past the car on the way to school and seeing him sleeping in it, but with as much fighting as he and my mother did, I felt it was better for him to be away from her anyway. They tell me that there was no way for me to know what was going on and that I shouldn't blame myself for not intervening and saving my father's life, but that didn't stop me from doing so on a daily basis. Even if I did, he probably would have found some other way to way to kill himself, one that I couldn't be around to witness. None of those details made me feel any better.

Grade school and high school were awful. I had no real friends, except for the occasional lab partner, but certainly no one that I would hang out with on weekends. It wasn't until I got to college that I began to have any kind of social life. Around my Junior year, I took a Music History class, largely at the insistence of my guidance counselor. It was incredibly boring and I probably wouldn't remember it at all, had I not met Danny in it. We were paired up on group projects frequently. When I confessed to him that I couldn't tell one composer or style of music from the other, he taught me tricks to try to bring me around. Sometimes they would help, but many times they would not. One day, in frustration, he said, "You have a brain in your head, don't you? Is your head filled with jelly beans?" Then he paused to realize what he just said. "Hmmm", he retorted, "Gloria Jean, the Jelly Bean!" And he smiled. His smile was so warm and bright that it lit a fire in my heart. Without even thinking, I slowly leaned over and kissed him. I had never kissed a man before who wasn't my father. If you think it surprised him, you should have seen how surprised it made me. I immediately pulled back and caught myself.

"Oh, my God!" shot out of my mouth.

"I have been accused of being a bad kisser before, but never to those extremes", he responded.

As I looked at my shoes, he took his index finger under my chin and raised my face until he was staring at me. He stared deeply into my eyes. He put his hand behind my right ear and slowly pulled my head toward his shoulder. Before I could think or react, I was deep in his arms. He was stroking my hair with his right hand.

"Do you have a boyfriend?" he questioned in low languid words.

He might as well have asked me if I had ever been on the moon.

"No", I stuttered. I was glad he didn't ask, "Have you *ever* had a boyfriend", because he may have been shocked to discover that the answer would have been the same. I should have known I was in way over my head based on his next response.

"You do *like* boys, don't you", he said I a comical way.

At that, I felt all the blood leave my head. I had just enough strength left to retort:

"*Some* boys."

He decided to have some fun with me in my hopeless situation.

"Do you see any boys around here that you like?" He said, as we glanced around the commons. "There are some nice guys on campus. Maybe I can introduce you so some of them." Then he hollered,

"Hey, guys, the Bean, here, is looking for a boyfriend…"

I hurriedly covered his mouth with my hand. I sheepishly said,

"I sorta like *you*!"

He looked so deep into my eyes that I felt like he hypnotized me. "You *sort of* like me, huh?" I shrugged and looked at my shoes.

"Well, we will have to give that matter some serious consideration, now won't we", he replied. What an answer! I would learn in the months and years to come, that Danny could make simple situations exceedingly profound with his charming repartee. Most of it he got from his grandmother, who was, to use one of her expressions, "as Irish as Paddy's Pig", whatever that meant.

As our relationship flourished, I came to realize that I loved Danny more than he loved me. I certainly loved Danny more than I loved myself, because I was plagued with the fact that, other than him, I had no life. My love for him turned into obsession, which made him become more distant, which led to me being more obsessed.

Danny liked to drink and I would drink along with him, but he could stop and I could not. I would drink until I was unconscious. It helped me to forget that I was the daughter of a suicide victim, and someone who felt like everyone "got it" but me. Drinking led to drugs and drugs led to drug addiction. I did my best to try to hide it. Maybe he could tell, maybe he couldn't, but one thing was clear – he was pulling away. I could tell that, before too long, I would only have one of the two things in my life; it would not be long before he would be out of the picture.

After graduation, it was apparent to me that our relationship was on its last gasp. That didn't stop me from trying to do everything I could to fan the flames yet again. He found some stupid job in a record store that sold old church music, or something. No one ever went in there. Danny went from there to the Irish bar down the street and from the bar to his dumpy apartment, and back to work to start the process all over again.

The Halloween party was supposed to be the thing that would bring us back together. Somewhere along the line, I got this hair-brained idea that he and his sisters played with Raggedy Ann dolls when they were all growing up, and that he had an affinity for them.

I talked him into taking me to the costume party at the trendy nightclub under the premise that I had a Raggedy Ann costume, which I did not. I convinced him to dress up as my male counterpart. It was a lot harder to make the costume than I thought it was going to be. As I tried making the costume and tried to do my hair and do my makeup, I got more and more nervous. This may have been my last chance to keep him in my life and everything was going wrong. My frustrations continued to build, all the time, thinking that dressing up like Raggedy Ann could rekindle the flames, which once existed between us. The more I thought about it and what was at stake the more nervous I became. This resulted in waves of despair, which led to tears, which led to me having to do and re-do my makeup, because my emotional outbreaks would wash it away time and again. The only way to keep my hair out of my eyes was to curl it tightly in big red ringlets. I rushed around for the last 45 minutes before he was supposed to pick me up, with far too many things to do and not enough time or desire to do them. The knock on the door sent panic through my heart. Would he like my costume? Would we stay together after this night? Did he still love me? I flung the door open, half hoping my latest scheme would work. He took one look at me and burst out laughing. I wanted to ask him what was so funny, when he recited a saying that his grandmother recited to him when she held him on her knee.

"Mother Mary Murgatroid, who curled your hair so tight?" shot out of his mouth.

I had no idea what that meant, as I rarely understood what most of the Irish wits and wisdoms that he professed meant, but it was so refreshing to see him so happy that I burst into laughter. Our laughter went on and on which finally led to us in a wild embrace. Why I never used birth control was beyond me. I think I thought that getting pregnant was something that happened to other people.

Despite my brilliant plan, he told me a couple of days later that he was about to change his life drastically and there was no place for me in it. My plans to save my relationship with the only man I ever loved blew up in my face. A month and a half later, I now found myself without him in my life and pregnant. The only thing to do was to break the news to him and hope that he would take me back. He was mad because I dragged him out of some sort of training class that he was in and, once again told me that there was no place for me in his "new" life. He did cobble up what little money he had and gave it to me, along with the phone book. It had the numbers of several abortion clinics circled. With Danny gone, my one and only companion was my addiction to drugs, which quickly led to heroine. Little did I know that a new companion was right around the corner.

Chapter Three
"Buttercup"

I am five year old. I don't like it that much. I almost never get to play or anything. I am with my mom most of the time. I think she is my mom. Kids at the park call their mom "mom". I call my mom Gloria Jean. Because that is her name. But no one else calls their mom by their first name. My name is Buttercup. I have never met anyone with my name before. Gloria Jean says that is my nickname. I don't know what that means. The kids at the park have last names. I guess I have a last name too, but I don't know what mine is. My eyes are dark brown and my hair is dark red. Some lady at the park once said I have knobby knees. I don't know that means, either. One time, two women were talking. One of them said I was "as cute as a button". I think that is good, because she smiled real nice when she said it. Lots of people say I am "dirty". That is because we have no bathtub. I wear the same clothes every day. Gloria Jean and I live in this old building with no windows, just wood over the window holes. It has chairs that are all face a stage in one big room. We don't go in there most times, through. It has rooms all over the place. Jelly Bean, that's my mother's nickname, kicked the back door in a long time ago. We snuck in. It's old and scary, but before that, we lived in a shelter. The old building is better than that. The shelter was hot and smelled bad. The people there would talk a lot to people who weren't there. What they did say made no sense. Old men would stare at me a lot and drool. There is a sink in the building we live in. Gloria Jean washes our clothes in it. Only sometimes, though, because sometimes it don't work all the time. If it's cold out, she doesn't, because our clothes have to sit on the roof to get dry. I have to sit with just underpants on and wait.

I wear the same light blue jumper and a white tee shirt every day. It was white once. Now, it is sort of gray. I don't have any toys, except a stuffed dog with no eyes. His name is Murgatroid. He is as dirty as me.

Sometimes, we could go to the park. Sometimes at the park, there were kids sitting in a circle. A woman with blond colored hair stood up and read to everyone from books. I loved listening to her read. I sat outside the circle once, but when she saw me, she stopped.

"Hello", she said. "I am Dorothy. Did you come to the Reader's Circle?" I shrugged my shoulders. "Is your mother nearby?" I turned and pointed to Gloria Jean on the bench. "Ask her if it is okay for you to join the circle".

I walked over to the bench. Gloria Jean was asleep, or something. I walked back. Dorothy was waiting and the other kids were looking at me.

"She said it was okay", I told her. Gloria Jean could see where I was, for when she woke up. Dorothy started reading about a boy who climbed up a beanstalk. I loved it when Dorothy read.

She got done with the book. She passed out crayons and coloring books for every one. I was surprised that I got one too, but I did. I opened the book. There was a picture of a boy on a wagon, but there were no colors. I opened the box of crayons and pulled out the red one. I started coloring all over the page. The boy next to me said:

"No, you Dope! You are doing it wrong!" I said:

"How do you do it?"

"Like this, you Nit-wit", and he started coloring the wagon brown. "Stay within the lines".

"I'm sorry!" I looked up and Dorothy was standing next to me.

"Oscar, that is very impolite. You shouldn't call other people names. You probably hurt her feelings". She looked at me. Her eyes were blue just like the sky. No one every looked at me like that before.

"What is your name, Sweetie?"

I didn't know what to say. Gloria Jean always said not to give my name to anybody. They might take me away if I did. I looked at my shoes.

"Ahh, no name…" I said every softly.

"Did you say Nola?" Dorothy put her hand on my shoulder. She talked real nice to me. I wanted to cry. I didn't. I nodded my head. "Well, Nola, tell your mother that we are here every day and you can come anytime you want". She rubbed the side of my head with her hand. It gave me the willies. She looked at the other kids and said "Color for 10 more minutes and then we will play make-believe". I didn't know what that meant. I guess I would have to wait to find out. I tried as hard as I could to keep my crayon marks inside the lines. I looked at the girl next to me to see how she colored and then tried to color the same way that she did. It was fun. I got up the courage to talk to the girl next to me. I said:

"Who taught you that?"

“Who taught me what?” She was not very nice.

“Who taught you how to draw like that?”

“What do you mean”, she said. “Everyone knows how to color”.

“They do?” I couldn’t believe it. “Have you colored before?”

“Of course I have”, she said, even meaner than before. “I got all sorts these at home, and good ones too, not these cheap ones”.

Even though she was mean to me, I thought of another question. “Do you have other toys at home, too?”

“Of course I do. My father’s an attorney”, she said.

“What does that mean?” I never heard that word before.

“He goes to court and makes it so people don’t have to go to jail”. She went back to her coloring.

Everyone was done but me. Dorothy said:

“Okay, everyone put your colors down. I would like to tell you about a game I played when I was little. It is a make-believe game. We would wait until it got dark and then we would look at the sky. When we saw the first star of the night we would say:

Star Light, Star Bright
First star I’ve seen tonight
I wish I may, I wish I might
Make this wish come true tonight

Then wish for something. If you are lucky and if you are very, very good, it will come true.”

Then it was time for Dorothy to go. Most kids left their crayons and books on the ground, so I picked them up and took them to Dorothy.

"Thank you, Nola. You are a very sweet girl. I shrugged my head. "May I see your drawing?" She smiled at me. I opened my book to the page that I colored.

"Sweetie, that is beautiful! You color very well". I shrugged my shoulders again. I thought my picture looked terrible compared to the other kids. Maybe Dorothy was just being nice.

I started to walk away. I thought of something. I turned back and Dorothy was still putting crayons in the box.

"Dorothy? Can I come back here…and color…and stuff some other time?" She looked confused.

"Nola, we are here every afternoon between 3:30 and 4:30. You are welcome any time". Then she smiled. "I will keep my eye out for you, Sweetie". She smiled another time when she said that. She was a real nice lady. I really liked her. I was real happy to get to talk to her, but I knew that in a minute, she was gonna go home and Gloria Jean was gonna wake up and I would have to go sit somewhere in an alley while she asked people for green money. So I was sad, too. I was happy but I was sad all at the same time. I didn't want Dorothy to go. I wanted to run over to her, and hug her and ask her if maybe I could be her little girl from now on or something but I didn't. I wished she could be my mom. But she couldn't. I have a mom. Maybe not a very good one, but I still have one. Besides, Dorothy probably had her own little girl at her house, a nice one, who could color real good already. She didn't need me, a dirty girl with no father hanging around her. But I knew how to fix that. Dorothy taught me how. I would wait until it got dark and went to one of the windows holes that had no wood on it. When I saw a star, I said.

Star lite, Star bite
First star eye cene tonight
I wisher may I wisher mite
Make this wish come true tonight

Then I held my breath. I thought I would wish for crayons and a book like Dorothy had, but that might be cheating. It might be two wishes. I wished I had new shoes and a new dress and toys but that might be a whole bunch of wishes. I thought I would wish for Dorothy to be my mom instead of Gloria Jean, but the wisher-guy might get mad if I wished for that. Then I thought I would just wish for Gloria Jean to be nice to me like Dorothy was. Maybe if I wasn't a dirty girl with no father, things would be different. But then I thought of it. I said:

I wish I had a father. Not a mean one, a nice one, who would buy me crayons and new clothes so that Gloria Jean wouldn't have to work so hard and so that Dorothy and everybody would think I was a nice girl.

So, that is what I did. That was sort of like more than one wish, but not really. If I got my wish and it helped Gloria Jean, too, the wisher-guy shouldn't be mad. I mean, it's not my fault that my wish would be good for Gloria Jean, too, was it?

Pretty soon, Gloria Jean came looking for me. It was time for me to get into the closet and to go to sleep. Then, it was the next day. We went back to the park, and sure enough, there was Dorothy reading stories to everyone. She read us stories about boys and pails of water and about gooses. She showed us pictures of them, too. They were in the book above the words.

When Dorothy got all done reading to us, it was time for everyone to go back to their houses. While I was putting my crayons away, I asked the girl next to me:

"Do you wish on a star?"

She looked at me mean.

"Ahh, NO, Dumb-bell! That is for BABIES!"

"Did you *ever* wish on a star?" I thought it was worth a shot.

"Well, yes when I was a BABY". She was meaner than before.

"What did you wish for", I asked.

"Well, you can't tell or it won't come true". She laughed after she said it. Her mother called her and she started walking toward her.

"Did *any* of your wishes come true? If they came true, you could tell then, couldn't you?"

She was almost to her mother when she answered. I was sort of following her, but not really.

"Oh, sure, lots of time", she said. "I wished for a swing set and I got it. I wished for a new bike and I got it. Lots of things". Then she got next to her mother. Her mother looked at me and smiled and said:

"Sheila, who is your friend?"

She looked at me. "Nola, right?" I shrugged. Her mother said,

"Why don't you ask Nola if she would like to come to our house to play?"

Sheila looked at me. "Well?"

"Ah, no thank you", I answered. I have to get home".

"Well, maybe some other time", her mother said. "It was nice to meet you, Nola." I shrugged my shoulders.

I was glad Sheila told me the rules. I was about to tell her what I wished for. Good thing I didn't. Sheila never came back to the park after that, but Dorothy did. She would always say,

"Bye bye, Nola. I hope you come back tomorrow". I hoped that I could. It made me feel like I was a normal kid. I loved the stories and Dorothy was teaching me how to read a little, too. I could see some of the words she read to us on billboard and signs in the windows.

Every day, Gloria Jean and I stood around on street corners. She asked people if she can borrow some green money from them. Gloria Jean slapped me once when I called her "mommy". It was when she made me stand in the alley a long time ago. She was "doing business". That is what she calls it. I got lonely standing there all by myself. She told me that I had to stay "out of sight". She said if "they realized what was going on", they would take me away. I didn't know who "they" were, or what was "going on". I didn't know where "away" was, but Gloria Jean said it was not a nice place. I believed her. I don't know why. Maybe because she was an adult and adults know things like that. She said that if they ever did take me away, I would probably never see her again. This one time Gloria Jean was asking a man for money. I got so lonesome that I walked over next to him. I pulled on his pant leg. When he looked down, I smiled at him. He was old and had gray hair. He sort of looked like Santa Claus.

"Is this little girl your daughter?" he snarled.

"Yes, it is, Sir! I am trying to get some money together so I can get her something to eat!"

"You should be ashamed of yourself" he bellowed, and reached into his wallet and gave Gloria Jean some green money. "I should call the authorities and turn you in!" He snorted.

"Oh, please, Sir, don't do that! She is the only thing I have in the whole world!" It was the first time she ever acted like she liked me.

Sometimes, I would do that again. Gloria Jean said the pant leg trick
worked great. It worked better on men, especially old ones. We began to call it our "sure-fire routine".

Sometimes, no one would give us money. We would still get hungry, though. Gloria Jean would put me in a closet in the building and say:

"Stay here. Don't make any noise. I will be back as soon as I can".

I hated being in that closet. It always seemed like I was in there forever. It probably wasn't that long though. When she came back, she brought food in wrappers. Sometimes, it smelled bad. She was dirtier than usual when that happened. The food was stale and not hot. I ate it anyway. If I didn't, I would have to stay hungry until morning, maybe longer.

On the corner, I would see big yellow buses go by. I asked Gloria Jean what they were, and where those kids on the buses were going. She said that those buses were full of good children, who had mothers and fathers and homes. Those children could afford to go to school. That made me wonder what I was. It made me wonder who my father was and where my father was and why did he let this woman make me stand around with her, night and day on this corner.

I think I would get in trouble if I asked. I asked Gloria Jean when I was going to get to go to school. She said:

"Some day maybe you can go, but not now". She didn't know about my secret. It wouldn't be that much longer, I thought. I made the same wish every night. Maybe it would be coming true soon. If Sheila's wish for a swing set would come true, the wisher-guy could make my father come back.

We slept in a room on the second floor of the building. She slept on the floor near the closet door. She made me sleep inside the closet. I didn't like it in there. I asked her why I had to sleep in there, and she said:

"If anyone finds us, they will find me and not you. The authorities would be mad enough if they catch me in here, but they would probably throw me in jail if they found me in here with you, and they would certainly take you away."

That must have been who the "they" were when we invented the "sure-fire routine". I still didn't understand what all of that "take you away stuff" meant, but it didn't sound so good.

When she fell asleep, I would look out of the crack in the closet door to see what she was doing. Lots of times I would see her with a glass tube and a lit match and a needle. She poked something in her arm with it. I couldn't really tell what was going on, but she sure seemed to feel better after it was all over.

Chapter 4
"Gloria Jean reaches out"

This whole thing was getting harder and harder all of the time. It was Spring, which made it easier to beg for money, but this was no way to live and certainly no way to be bringing up a little girl. She should be sleeping in a bed, eating breakfast cereal out of a bowl and, most importantly, she should be going into First Grade in the Fall. I was constantly in a bad mood, largely because of my drug addiction. I should be more loving to my little girl, but every time I looked at her, she reminded me of how I got my heart broken by her father. I tried to stay as distant as I could from her, for that reason, but there was something more: I was always afraid that someone would discover that I was raising a child on the street and would take her away from me. I might not miss her so much if I pretended not to love her in the first place. That sounds pretty selfish, but hey, I am a drug addict raising a 5 year old on the streets of New York City. It is the best logic I could muster up. Then there was something else going on, too and it was just as bad. I was in no hurry for her to wrap her little head around the fact that her mother was some pitiful bag lady either.

Even if I could keep my wits about me long enough to enter her into public school, I knew that continuing the charade would be impossible. They would want personal information like my address. I couldn't very well tell them I lived in an abandoned vaudeville theatre. Public education is free, but they would want some money for school supplies and stuff like that, which I didn't have. Any money I was able to scrape together was either used to try to feed us, or went up my arm in a syringe. I felt worse and worse all the time. There was a dull thud in my head most of the time. Sometimes I heard a ringing in my ears, which went on for hours. Occasionally, I heard people talking to me, but when I turned around, they were gone.

There was a free clinic, where I used to take Buttercup, my daughter, every once in a great while when she had serious diseases, like chicken pox. They always wanted to ask me too many questions, like "Has your daughter received her MMR shots?" or "Who is the girl's regular doctor?" I knew that keeping a low profile would be the only way to keep them from taking Buttercup away from me.

I started sleeping until the late afternoon, then not having enough energy to pan-handle to try to get money for food. Buttercup would wander around the old theatre, usually in the dark. She would be hungry by the time I woke up and she could easily have gotten hurt running around in this old building. I also worried that she would wander outside and get spotted by the police or get abducted by some local creeper. It was time for me to go see one of these "loser doctors" that either couldn't get a better job in a nice hospital or who were just starting their career and had to work their way up. What the doctor told me was no surprise. He said I had developed a chemical dependency to a dangerous drug. What I was surprised to learn is that he gave me about 6 months to live, unless I radically changed my life habits. It was obvious to him that I was indigent. He took a brochure out of his desk drawer that spoke of a program that was free of charge. The patients would live in a locked-down facility for up to 3 months. They would be given drugs to lessen the withdrawal symptoms, and eventually wean them off of whatever it was they were addicted to. There were also classes about dealing with your feelings, and that sort of stuff; life skills designed to teach you how to lead a productive life. I didn't care one way or the other about that. All I wanted to do was to make this thud in my head stop. The "loser doctor" told me that the program was accepting applicants and would start their next session in 3 days. He told me that only 36 people were admitted at a time and there were 32 on the list. He had all the necessary paperwork that I would need to fill out, which I did with him sitting across the desk from me. I figured out that if it didn't save my life, it might turn out to be "3 hots and a cot" for 3 months.

As I was filling out all of these ridiculous forms, a thought jumped into my head. "That sounds fine, Doctor, but is there a separate place for the children or would my daughter stay with me? After all, if I am going to go through withdrawals, I would rather she not have to go through it with me."

The doctor looked puzzled. "You can't have children in the program. How old are your children?"

I was secretly afraid that he would say that.

"It is just one child, a little girl. She is 5 years old."

"Can you make other arrangements for her care while you are in the dependency unit? Maybe she could stay with your mother", he said.

That was about the funniest thing I had ever heard. I may not have been a candidate for mother of the year, but Buttercup would be dead if I left her in the care of my mother. My mother, God rest her wicked soul, was drunk by 2:00 O'clock in the afternoon and the house could burn down around her head and she would never wake up.

I reluctantly said "Do they ever make exceptions? She really is no trouble! She can eat some of my food and sleep in my bed…"

The doctor stopped me in mid sentence. "First of all, if she is 5 years old, she should be in Kindergarten anyway. The state would never allow her to miss all of that time from school. Second, you can't have any of the worldly distractions from your daily life following you there. If you can't make other arrangements, I will have to no longer consider you as a candidate for the program".

I saw this as my last chance. In a panic, I said, "I can get my mother-in-law to take her. Please don't kick me out of the program". That would have been a good trick, seeing as how I didn't have a mother-in-law.

I was told to report to the clinic on Monday at 1:00 PM. This being Friday at 4:00PM didn't give me a lot of time to formulate any massive schemes.

I spent most of Saturday ignoring the situation. Finally on Sunday, I had to level with Buttercup. I took her to the park that she liked to go to and let her swing on her favorite swing for longer than usual. It was sunny spring day, the kind of day best not occupied with bad news. But that, unfortunately, was not to happen. It was time for me to break the news to her.

"Let's go sit on the bench, I have to talk to you about something", I said.

"Honey, I am sick. I have to go into the hospital for a while."

Buttercup's little face got a twisted, worried look on it.

"Do you have the Chicken Pox?" she asked

"No, honey, it is nothing like that. But I do have to go into the hospital for about 3 month, maybe longer."

"Will I go too?'' she sheepishly questioned.

"No you can't. They don't allow children".

"Will I stay in the building by myself?" she asked.

"No, it would be too dangerous", I told her. "There would be no one to take care of you". My point seemed so ridiculous, because I didn't really take very good care of her in the first place.

Buttercup looked at her shoes. In the tiniest voice I had ever heard her speak in, she said "well, what will happen to me?"

"Well", I answered, "I had been thinking about that. I spoke with your father and he will take care of you until I get out. Then things will be much better. I will get a job, you will go to school and we won't have to live in that theatre anymore".

Buttercup started to cry, "My father?"

"It will only be for a little while", I said. Now, tears were streaming down my face, as well.

"…But I want to stay with you", she whimpered. Her eyes, filled with big blobs of tears, slowly rose until she was looking into my eyes.

"…But you will get to meet your father", I whimpered out myself, stifling back my own tears.

"What if I don't like my father", she asked between sniffles.

"I think you will. He is a very successful man and he can buy you lots of new things".

"But I don't want new things. I want to stay with you. Mommy…"

She caught herself in mid syllable. She was waiting to get slapped. I foolishly slapped her face once before for calling me "mommy". It was when I was asking some guy for money. She was tired and wanted to go home. It was a day I will never forget, as long as I live. She looked at me and said, "Mommy, are we going home soon?" I guess that is the day I realized that I really was somebody's mother and that I was doing a pretty miserable job of it. I was so startled by the awfulness of the situation that I did the unthinkable. I slapped her across the face. As soon as I did it, I regretted it. She didn't do anything that any other child might have done in such a situation. I could tell that she was more hurt emotionally than physically. I guess I did what I did because I didn't want her to think that her "mother" was some disheveled bag lady, so I always trained her to call me by my first name.

I was shocked back into the present by what Buttercup said next. "I'm sorry", she whimpered.

I wanted to reach out and hold her, but it seemed very unnatural. "What are you sorry for?", I retorted.

"For being bad…I am sorry that I am one of the bad children, with no father who can't go to school." Her little voice was breaking my heart.

"No sweetheart, you haven't done anything bad. Actually, I have been bad. I have done things that I shouldn't have".

"I don't care if you did something bad", she replied.

"Honey, don't think about it like you are getting punished. Think about it like a brilliant new experience". At that, I did something I hadn't done in years. I picked her up and put her in my lap.

"Mommy….can Murgatroid come to meet my dad, too?"

"Of course he can", I comforted.

"Mommy…..are you going to die?"

"I don't think I am", was the only thing I could think of.

"Mommy….you are hugging me too tight".

I didn't even realize it. I was holding her so tightly, I am surprised she could breathe. I held her like I may never see her again – because that might be true.

"I am sorry, honey." I rocked her back and forth in my lap, like she was a new-born baby. Before I knew it, I could hear that she was fast asleep. I picked her up carried her back to the abandoned theatre. Now, the only thing left to do was to tell Danny he had to take care of Buttercup. But first, I had to tell him that he was a father.

Chapter 5
"Monday Morning"

“Danny, your 4:30 has to meet with you earlier. They are leaving for the West Coast at 4” Toodles bellowed from the door.

My secretary was highly efficient, very well organized and treated everything like the building was on fire. Her real name was Towanda Harrison, but no one, including her own mother, called her anything but Toodles. The only thing crazier than Mondays in the investment banking business was Mondays in the springtime. Everyone suddenly realized that they have to get their portfolios in shape before they could go the “the shore” or wherever rich people went all summer. That type of bedlam made Toodles crazier and more frenetic than usual. Now, in addition to all of the regular stuff there was the “Monday morning – Oh, My God, I didn’t plan for that” stuff.

Toodles was on a rip. “I picked up your shirts at the dry cleaner…for the *last time*. You have a meeting at 10:00, which translates into 15 minutes from now. *That means* you have to *shave*. While you are at it, get your *feet* off of your *desk*”.

“Well, since you have taken over the firm, is there anything else I can do for you?” I snarled.

“Yes, there is. You could you tell that skanky ex-girlfriend of yours to quit calling here collect!”

“Which skanky ex-girlfriend would that be”? I retorted.

“The only one who can’t afford to drop a quarter in a pay phone. Gloria Jean”.

“I hadn’t heard from ‘the Bean’ in months”, I replied. The last time was last fall when she needed money to buy winter clothes. I should state that every time she calls it is because she needs money for something.

"Well, what did she want?" I asked.

"Well, I don't *know* that, now do I? I would have had to *accept* the charges to *do that*", Toodles snapped. Many people wouldn't put up with her attitude, but I did because at the base of it, I knew that she was a fighter and what I needed was a fighter in my corner. For that matter, most secretaries wouldn't put up with as much of the nonsense as I dished out, anyway.

"Well, if she calls again, accept the charges..."

"Danny...."

"Just, do it, Toodles! Tell her I am in a meeting and find out what she wants".

I forgot all about the most recent 'Gloria Jean' citing until almost 11:00. As I went from one meeting to another, the trusty Toodles was there with a cup of coffee for me, as well as a handful of messages.

"The 4:00 has to meet at 3:30 and Jackson wants to reschedule for later in the week". Toodles rattled off. "The people from 'Haines, Warrington' need an answer on your proposal specs and you have 3 more hours before the Hanford deal disappears". She went on. "Oh, and one more thing. Gloria Jean called back. I *accepted* the charges, like you *told* me to. She would like you to meet her at Galagher Park at 12:00".

There is no way I could meet with the president of the United States today with my schedule, much less some long-lost girlfriend from six years ago. Over my shoulder, I told Toodles, "If she calls back, tell her I am out of town and I will deal with it when I get back."

"That's not gonna work this time, Danny. She sounded real bad! She was crying...real hard!"

I wondered what kind of trouble she got herself into this time. I just hoped that, whatever it was, that it didn't spell trouble for me. As I was closing the door on the conference room, I said, "If you can remind me at 11:45 and have a taxi standing by, I can swing down there, give her a couple hundred bucks and be back here by 12:30", half to Toodles and half to myself.

"Danny, when am I gonna find time…" Toodles started to say.

"11:45! And get two hundred dollars out of my ATM!
Thank you, Toodles".

Toodles gave me a look that could curdle milk.

After a meeting that could only be compared to as a root channel, Toodles knocked at the conference room door.

"Mr. Cullen, it's 11:45. Your car is waiting downstairs. Here are those papers you requested," said Toodles, as she handed me an envelope. There were no papers, the envelope was stuffed with 20 dollar bills. She was always professional in front of clients. It was when it was just her and I that she assumed that I worked for her.

"Thank you, Toodles. Gentlemen, I will see you next Wednesday, with new proposals. GLG appreciates your business", I said as I walked out of the room and down to the street. My next serious task was to see if two hundred dollars would be enough to keep the past the past and my little secret a secret.

Chapter 6
"Buttercup's Response"

Gloria Jean let me call her "Mommy". That was different. It was strange, too. It was almost like someone saying that dogs were

really named cats. It was almost as though someone told me Murgatroid was really a cat. Guess what else was weird? She took me to the park in the middle of the day. She never did that before. There were all of these other kids all running around. Some I knew from Dorothy, but others I didn't.
They chased each other. One kid was "it" and he did the chasing. Then he tagged a slow kid and then the slow kid was "it". I started running around and pretty soon I was "it". Some of the kids were mean to me. One boy kept calling me "Stinky", but most of them were pretty nice, I guess.

The only person I had known my whole life was Glor-""Mommy". Now, she was sick. I didn't know how she got sick or anything. Maybe I was sick, too. If I was, would I get everyone around me sick? Would I get Dorothy sick? And what was all this business about my father? Was my wish coming true? I had to go live with him now. It had to be better than living in that old building. Maybe he had some toys that he would let me play with. I wondered if he stood on a different corner and asked different people for money. I asked Gloria Jean about a million questions on the way to the park:

"What if I don't like him? What does he look like? Is he mean? Does he like kids?" Every time I thought I had no more questions, another one popped into my head. Gloria Jean didn't answer hardly none of them. All I could think about was I probably wouldn't ever see her again, at least maybe for a long, long time.

Once I got to the park, I stopped thinking about it. Playing on the Monkey-bars sure beat standing downtown watching my mother ask men for green money. And I really wasn't gonna to use up any of my swing-set time on "daddy" questions.

I could see Gloria Jean sitting on a bench. It was far away, but I could still see her okay. I saw a man walk over by her. There were no stars out, but I wished it again anyway, just in case. He sat on the bench next to her. She talked to him for a long time. She shot up and quickly walked over to me. She was crying. I hate it when people cry. It makes me want to cry just looking at them. She walked over and sat on the swing next to me. She said:

"Stay right here on this swing. You will meet your father soon. I love you, Buttercup! I always have!"

Tears rolled down her face. She was so sad, it made me cry too.

"I am sorry I wasn't a better mother to you", she said. "Please believe me, Sweetheart, I did the best I could. When I come back, things will be better! It will be…it will be…" She was so sad, she couldn't talk. She got off the swing and went flying back over by the man on the bench. She sat back down next to him. Then, she got up and ran away. I was alone. I was all alone in this park. Gloria Jean was gone. Maybe forever. I felt sick. If I could jump off the swing and chase her, I would, but I can't reach the ground. After a little while, the man got up and started to walk toward me. Then I looked at my shoes.

Chapter 7
"Gloria Jean's Secret"

"Danny, I need a favor from you", I said through my tears.

"Bean, I am SO running behind today. I have 200 dollars for you. I hope that it is enough. If you need more, I will tell Toodles to have more for you by the end of the day", Danny said, sticking an envelope into my ribs.

"Danny, I don't need any money". I never said that to anyone before in my life.

"Danny, you have to do something for me". I said "I have to go to the hospital. The doctor says I may die if I don't".

"What's wrong?" Danny had genuine concern in his voice when he said that. "Are you okay?'

"It is a drug dependency clinic. The doctor said I have to get clean or I am going to die!" My words scared me as much as they did him.

"Well, maybe I can con my insurance company into thinking we are married and get them to pay for it", he said in a forgiving manner.

"No, it is the not the money", I told him. "The state will pay for it…but there is something I have to tell you". He looked at me with the most confused look I had ever seen.

"Remember when I got pregnant?"

"Don't you mean to say 'do I remember when I GOT you pregnant'?" he quipped.

"Danny, please, let's not fight now".

"I gave you money for that, Gloria!"

"Danny…I didn't…I didn't…I…"

"Gloria, you didn't…what?"

"Danny, I didn't have the abortion". Danny flung his head wildly.

"I have to report to the clinic today…now…I am probably late as it is. But I can't take my daughter…our daughter…into the hospital with me…you have to take her! Danny, you have to take care of *our daughter* until I get out."

Danny's face turned white. He fidgeted back and forth and shuffled from side to side with his feet. He let a little snide smirk come over his face.

"That's funny, Gloria! You always did know how to make me laugh, didn't you?"

"Danny, I am serious! I am deadly serious!" I peered into his eyes, trying to make him understand just how much trouble I was in.

"So, let me get this straight," Danny continued. "I am supposed to believe…that you…HAD that baby? That is impossible!" He shot his hand through his hair. "You have been living on the street for…" A light bulb seemed to go on in his head. "Are you telling me that you have been raising a child…on the streets….for 5 years?"

"Well," I interjected, "now that you put it that way, I guess that just about sums it up!"

"So, I am supposed to believe this, huh?"

"Supposed to believe *what,* Danny?"

"I am supposed to believe that I have a kid somewhere…"

I interrupted him. "Not *somewhere,* Danny*! There!"* I pointed to the swing. *Her* name is Barbara Danielle McCullen, but I have been calling her 'Buttercup'. See, when she was a baby, couldn't pronounce Barbara and....

Danny violently interrupted me. "I get it. You are in this great big 'world of hurt' and now you want to make your little trouble, be *my* trouble, huh? Well, guess what? I don't believe it!"

I was hoping that this wasn't going to turn into the Jack Dempsey fight, but I could see that it was way too late for that.

"Well, how about this one? It isn't *my* problem and it isn't *your* problem…it is *our* problem! And whether you believe it or not, or like it or not, it is true…and it is happening…and it is happening to *you*!" Under my breath, I added, "and it is happening to *me*…and it is happening to *her!"*

"So, I supposed I just have to take your word for all of this, huh?" Danny was not happy. "You know, I am not all that surc that that baby was mine in the first place!" Whether he meant that or not was hard to say. He acted like a man who was desperately trying to come up for air. Regardless of his intentions, I was furious.

"You Bastard", I screamed. "You self-absorbed, conceited bastard! I may be a lot of things Daniel McCullen, but unfaithful is *certainly* not one of them!"

There was an awkward silence while we stood there and looked at each other.

"Look, Danny, this sucks, I know that. I am not happy about this and I wish I wasn't here asking for this, but I am. I need you to take Buttercup…*please*, just until I get out of rehab". I tried to make light of it with a smile, but I just sniffled instead". "I swear, Danny, if you do this for me, I will come back and get her and you never see me again…ever! I will never bother you again! I will never ask you for money again…but I need this….and I need it now!"

"Gloria, it is not that I *don't* want to help you, but what do I know about raising a child?"

"Danny, you are a God-forsaken Millionaire! You make Wall Street rise and fall every day. How hard could this be? Jesus, Danny, you could get Toodles to do it for you; she practically runs your whole life as it is".

Danny looked into my eyes and then he looked at the ground.

"I swear to God, Gloria, if you don't come back…Let's go meet my daughter."

A sick feeling came over me. This was it. This was really going to happen. The only thing that meant anything to me, the only thing that I had was about to be gone…and I was about to be all alone.

"I can't do it, Danny; I can't walk over there". Danny looked confused.

"Alright", he said. "I'm finished playing around. Do you want me to take her or not?" Danny was getting agitated and annoyed.

"I do, Danny…but…You have to go get her…I can't…I can't look her in the eyes again and…" I swallowed hard. "Here is her birth certificate, and all of the records I have about her…" I handed a wad of paperwork to Danny. "I have to go Danny. Please, I am counting on you…PLEASE take care of her until I am well enough to do it myself!"

My ears were ringing and everything seemed like a dream. I knew if I didn't get up and leave, I would never be able to do it. I jumped up and ran out of the park, leaving Danny to stare at the swings and Buttercup to stare at her shoes.

Chapter 8
"Danny Meets Buttercup"

I looked at the swing-set that were about fifty feet away. There was a little girl on the swing that was all the way on the left. The swing was barely moving because her feet didn't reach the ground and she had no way to get herself started. I took the mish-mash of papers that Gloria Jean gave me and stuck them in my pocket. I looked to my left and then to my right, but there was no one in the park that I knew. It was just me and a gaggle of kids and a little girl on a swing. A strange sound kept going on then off, on then off. I couldn't figure out what it was. After the sound went off for the 6th time, it occurred to me what it was; it was my cell phone. It stopped.

Walking over to the swing, I wondered what I would say. Was this kid really my daughter? What kind of kid would she be? Would she be some "Demon Child" that would kill me in my sleep? The little "Devil" voice in me said:

"Leave! No one knows who you are! Hi-tail it out of there! Get out while you still can!"

I didn't. Instead, I continued to walk toward the swings. When I got right in front of it, I saw what had to be the exact copy of what Gloria Jean must have looked like when she was that age, whatever age that was. She was still looking at her shoes.

"Hello". Not a great beginning for a man who meets his daughter for the first time, but it was all I could think of.

She wouldn't look up.

"I'm Danny". I tried to sound reassuring.

"I know", her little voice whined. "Gloria Jean told me." She seemed racked with fear.

There was a long pause. We were both speechless. Finally, she broke the silence.

"Gloria Jean is coming back for me, you know". She never raised her eyes as she made this proclamation. I resisted the urge to say, "…and that can't happen soon enough for the likes of me", but that didn't seem to be the way I wanted this relationship to begin. Instead, I said:

"I know". I was struck at how my answer was the same as hers. We have known each other for 30 seconds and we were already starting to talk like each other.

"How long do I have to stay with you at your house?" Her eyes finally looked up at me.

"Gee", I answered, "I don't know. I guess until your mom can take care of you herself".

"She's not…" her voice trailed off, as she didn't finish her sentence. "Where do you live?" Now she was staring at me. Her little face was beautiful. She was certainly Gloria Jean's daughter.

"Not very far from here", I said. "I have sort of a big Condo. It has…3?...4?...5? bedrooms (I had to count them in my head, because I hardly ever go in any of them). We can make one of them be your bedroom if you like."

"Do you have other little kids living in your *big condo*?" She sort of mimicked the way I said it.

"No, you will be the first", I answered.

"Well, why do you have so many bedrooms if you don't have any other kids?"

"I don't know", I told her. "I guess that is how many bedrooms it came with".

"Do you have a bath tub?" She must have wanted to hear the whole layout of my house before she would agree to the new living conditions.

"Yes, I do", I answered. "I have three bathtubs".

"Does your wife take a lot of baths?" Barbara seemed fascinated by the whole bath tub thing.

"I don't have a wife", I told her.

"Well, who takes baths in all of those bath tubs?" She was a little exasperated.

"Well, *you are* when we get you home!" I stopped short of commenting on her filthy face and stained clothes.

"Do I have to come?" There was worry in her voice.

Again, I was torn as to how to respond. "Well, what else would you do?" I was trying to reason with a 5 year old. After she thought about it, she said:

"Could I just stay here…in the park?"

It was time to be the adult. "No, Sweetie, you couldn't."

"Why? I like the park." Her face was full of fear. It was time for me to change strategies.

"Because the bear that sleeps in the park would bite your toes *all night* and you wouldn't get any sleep". There had to be some practical reason for being Irish and having the ability to make up goofy stories, and this was one of them. As she looked up, she smirked.

"There aren't any *bears* living in the park!" Even she could see through my ridiculous story, but it made her laugh.

I leaned into her. "How do *you* know?" I said as ridiculously as I could.

"*Because',* she was said exasperated. "Bears live in the Zoo!"

"Yeah", I continued. "Well, maybe *this one escaped*!

She was laughing pretty hard at the bear story. There was another long silence. Finally, the little conversationalist broke the silence yet again.

"Did you ever wish on a star?" She squinted as she looked up at me. I thought that was a pretty obscure questions, but if that was what she wanted to talk about, I figured it was better than the two of us standing there saying nothing.

"You mean 'Star Light, Star Bright'? That wising on a star? Sure I did, when I was younger". She seemed resolute about my answer.

"It's for babies, you know", she said as she wrinkled her nose.

"Not really", I replied. "What made you think of that?"

"I don't know". She seemed like she was through with that topic.

In what seemed like her first act of testing this new relationship, she looked to her left. "I haven't gone on the monkey-bars yet", she rattled off.

"We don't really have time for that today", I reasoned. "I have to get back to the office. Let's get your stuff".

"Stuff?" Her little face got confused.

"Well, yes", I continued. "Your clothes and stuff".

“I got him”, she said, looking at a raggedy old stuffed dog that was sitting on her lap.

Searching for things to say, I asked “Who’s that?”

Murgatroid”, she said. “He is my dog. He is not a real dog, but almost. He can come too, can’t he?” Gloria Jean must have told her about the Halloween party.

“Well, of course he can, but where your clothes?”

“I’m WEARING them”, she said in an exasperated voice.

“No! Your other clothes”, I continued.

“I don’t have…” her voice trailed off.

“Well, you must have other clothes, right”? I looked around for a suitcase.

“No. No other clothes”, she said, shaking her head.

“Wait…are you trying to tell me that the only clothes you own are the ones you are wearing?” I couldn’t believe what I was hearing.

“Yes”. Her head dropped back down to her shoes.

“No toys? No…nothing?” My voice heated up.

“No”. She seemed ashamed of herself.

“Wait a second” I bellowed. “I have to talk to Gloria Jean”, I said practically screaming. “What is the name of the hospital she is in?”

“I don’t know”. Her little voice answered like someone who got caught doing something bad. I obviously hurt her feelings. I took a long breath and composed myself.

“I’m sorry, Sweetie! I’m sorry if I yelled at you! This isn’t your fault! You didn’t do anything wrong…I’m just…well…”

“It’s okay”, she said, letting me off the hook.

“It looks like after work today, we…you and I…are going to have to go to the store and buy you clothes…and from the sound of it, we will have to buy you LOTS of clothes”. That seemed to cheer her up. “But we do have to go now”, I said, in my best dad-comforting voice. I didn’t have much practice with that voice. I would have to work on that if I were to care for a child for the next 3 months. “Why do they call you Buttercup?” I asked, as I grabbed her under the arms and lifted her off of the swing.

“I don’t know”, she answered, and her feet plopped down on the ground. “Dorothy calls me Nola”.

“Who is Dorothy?” I was a little bewildered.

“The lady in the park”, she answered.

“Who is Nola? I mean, why does she call you Nola?”

“Well”, she thought for a long time. “I guess…I don’t know”.

“Well, I think I will call you Barbara for now”. Don’t ask me how I arrived at that decision. Perhaps, I was afraid that Buttercup had some sort of drug reference attached. Maybe I wanted to strike a different kind of relationship with Barbara than the one she and her mother had.

"What am I supposed to call you?" Her question was a good one. After all, what she didn't know about me was exactly as much as I didn't know about her. I struggled with having her call me Dad, but that might not be the best idea. Mr. Cullen seemed way too formal.

"Tell you what, for now, why don't you just call me Danny", I answered. "Did you have lunch yet?"

"We didn't have enough money for lunch *or* breakfast", she said. "I didn't get any dinner last night, either".

"Well, you must be starving. Let's start by getting you something to eat." I said, starting toward the trail that led out of the park.

"Won't we have to stop and ask people for some green money first?" She said looking up at me.

A little dumbfounded, I said "Ahh…no, I have my own *green* money".

I made a decision, right then and right there. I made the decision that this relationship was going to work and it was going to work because I was going to make it work. I was a little nervous, but I said,

"Barbara? Can we hold hands?" She swallowed hard. There was a little tear forming in her eye and she looked scared.

"Do we have to?" Her voice was full of trepidation.

"We don't *have* to" I stammered… "but I would *like* to".

"Well", she answered. "I don't usually hold hands. I'm not a baby, you know!"

“I know you are not a baby, but I like to hold hand”, I said. “One time, I held hands with a porcupine for two hours.

Barbara laughed. “You did not!”

“Ahh, yes I did”, I figured the more goofy stories I would tell her, hopefully she wouldn’t just see me as some man in a suit. “His name was Peter Porcupine. He is quite the convivial fellow”. I knew that she wouldn’t know what convivial meant, but that sounded silly and most kids like silly.

She had no answer.

“See, here is the thing”, I began. “If you got lost, I would be terrified! I would probably sit down and start to cry!” At that, I made big, silly sobbing sounds and began rubbing my eyes. That made Barbara laugh. “*But*! If we held hands, you *can’t* get lost and I *won’t* start crying and…”

At that, Barbara began to laugh so hard that the people around us began to notice us. Those people included a very large policeman, who walked up behind Barbara.

“Excuse me, sir! Do you have any identification?” He said, as he put his hands on his hips.

A little dumbfounded, I said “Gee, Officer, I didn’t know I needed I.D. to take my *daughter* to the park. Do they have laws against that?”

“They do if you aren’t her father”, he said in a belligerent tone. Barbara turned her back to me. Now, she was facing the cop.

“Oh, trust me, Officer, I *am* her father”. Barbara’s head snapped back to look at me when I said this.

“I see her in this park a lot, and I see her bag-lady mother, but I never see you…you, with your fancy suit”, he said as ran his fingers under the lapel of my jacket.

“Crappy lawyer”, I said, trying to work up a little giggle. “Sullivan, huh?” I said, reading his name badge. “My name is McCullen. I probably sat next to your cousin in grade school”. That is the great thing about being Irish, everyone thinks they are related to you. I pulled out my driver’s license and handed it to the cop.

“You may have”, the cop answered. “He was the world’s biggest drunk! Why does your driver’s license say your name is Cullen?”

“Oh, one of those Ellis Island snafus”, I said with a chuckle.

“Do you have any form of identification for her?” he said looking at her.

“As a matter of fact, Officer, I have her birth certificate right here”.

“Convenient”, he said, as I handed him badly-worn document. “Why would you be carrying her birth certificate around with you?

I felt like saying “you ask me for identification and when I produce it, you ask me why I have it?” but that line of argument seemed like it would provoke a very unpleasant response from him. “I *have it* because her mother has to go into the hospital and I am going to care for her until she gets out. She felt I might need it for such an occasion as we are having right now”.

“Funny you bringing her mother up”, the cop retorted. “We have been keeping our eyes on her *and* her mother for a while now. Her mother pan-handles almost every day, and that little girl is usually sitting in an alley waiting for her”.

"Well, that is all about to change, Officer. I am an investment planner and am pretty good at it. I make lots of money and I have lots of money and I am going to be taking care of her from now on. You won't see her or her mother, probably ever again".

"Good", he said, "because we were about to run her mother in and have Child and Family Services investigate. However, I guess that won't be necessary now. Have a nice day, Sir". He handed me my driver's license and Barbara's birth certificate back and walked away.

He turned one way and Barbara and I turned the other. We started walking out of the park.

As we started to walk down the path, I bent over slightly and said to Barbara: "That was a close call, huh?" I was still a little shaken by the whole event. Trying to change the subject, I said, "Have you given any more thought to that holding hands stuff?" At that, Barbara spun around and looked back in the direction of the policeman.

"Hey, Copper", her voice rang out from behind me. Sullivan turned around. "My dad holds hands with porcupines". There was a smile on her face, as she hid behind my legs, taunting the cop. Keeping my gaze fixed on the cop, I tried to quiet Barbara down.

As soon as the cop was out of range, I swung around and got on one knee.

"Barbara, that was impolite. That man thought you might be in trouble and he was trying to help you!"

The smile dissolved from her face.

"I'm sorry", she whimpered, as she looked at her shoes. I won't be bad anymore."

"It's okay, it happens", I responded. I straightened up and started walking with Barbara at my side back down the trail.

"Were you ascared?" Her question surprised me. I couldn't tell if she changed the subject or if she was actually asking me a question.

"Ascared? Of what?", I responded.

"When that cop was asking you all of them questions ", she answered.

"No…well, a little", I stammered out. "But, that doesn't matter. I am with you now, and I could face a lot tougher than that big, dumb cop Irish…for you".

Without another word, I felt a tiny, little hand take mine. It was the most wonderful thing I remember feeling in years.

Chapter 9
Breakfast

The first restaurant we came to was a "Ham-n-egger, all night diner" that has 200 things on the menu and everything tastes the same.

"Would you like to eat here?" I asked. She shrugged.

A short, squatty man met us at the door wearing a dirty undershirt.

"Oh, no you don't! You don't come in here with that kid!" and he reached out to grab her. I intercepted his hand and positioned myself between him and her.

"You touch her and I swear to God, I'll bust your head wide open", I screamed. My actions were so visceral that they startled Barbara.

"That kid and her mother are always eating out of my dumpster, always trying to get free stuff from me! Always stealing silverware and salt shakers", the greasy guy said.

"Well I don't want anything for free and I have my own salt shakers!" At that, I pulled a wad of 20 dollar bills out of the envelope I had for Gloria Jean and waved them in the air. "Will *this* get us a seat in here?'

"That is *different*" the man retorted. "Phyllis, get these two a table".

I wanted to ask Barbara what that was all about, but I figured she would just shrug anyway.

As we sat down at the table, I asked "What do you want to eat? I used that fatherly voice I had been working on. She looked up from her menu and shrugged. "Do you want breakfast or lunch?" Again, she shrugged. It was obvious I was not going to get a straight answer out of her. I was going to have to make some decisions on my own. By now, the waitress showed up.

"Don't mind him" she spewed out. "He has been in a bad mood for 20 years. Hey it's...that kid…the one with the name like the flower". She obviously recognized Barbara. "…why is she…who are…? Hey, what's going on here, Mister? Who are you?"

"Why do you just call me Nunya", I snapped back.

"Nunya?" Her tone was as snotty as his.

"Yeah, Nunya Business! We came in here to get something to eat, not to play 20 questions"

"Yeah", she spouted back, "Suppose I just call the cops!" She wasn't about to give up.

"Well, suppose you do", I snapped back, "Ask for Officer Sullivan, because I just had this same conversation with him, now can we order our food?" At that I laid 3 20 dollar bills in the table.

""Well, I guess there is no need for the police", she said backing down. She must have taken me for a big tipper.

I looked across the table and said "Barbara, do you know what you want?"

"No, not really", her little voice squeaked out.

"Do you want breakfast or lunch?"

"I don't know", she said in a sheepish voice.

"Do you like eggs?" I said.

"Maybe. I don't know. I don't think I have ever had eggs before."

The waitress couldn't believe it. "What kind of kid never ate eggs before?" She snorted.

"MY kid…! And don't forget, *you* work for *tips*! The young lady will have two scrambled eggs." I said.

"Two scrambled eggs" the waitress replied.

"Two poached eggs" I said.

"Wait, Pal, do you want two scrambled eggs or two poached eggs?" She said impatiently.

"Both. And two eggs Sunny Side Up, and an order of Eggs Benedict", I said, as I stared at Barbara, who wouldn't look up from the menu.

"Anything else?" She bellowed.

"Yes, an order of bacon" I instructed.

"Bacon", the waitress said, writing it down on her pad.

"And an order of sausage…." I added.

"Bacon *and* sausage", she said in a snide voice, "Links or patties" the waitress asked.

"Both", I said, never taking my eyes off Barbara, who wouldn't take her eyes off of the menu.

"Two eggs scrambled, two poached eggs, two eggs up and Eggs Benedict. Bacon, sausage links and patties. Anything else?" Her belligerent voice continued.

"Yes, pancakes…,and waffles…and French Toast". I said. "and bring all of the syrup you can find back there.

"Who is going to eat all of this?" She snorted.

"Just worry about who is going to pay for it", I belted out, pointing to the 20 dollar bills on the table. "I tip big", I said under my voice. Her mood changed.

"And to drink?" she asked.

"Apple juice…tomato juice…grapefruit juice…." I trailed on.

"*Orange* juice?" The waitress chimed in.

"Yes, and milk". I answered.

"Chocolate or regular?" the waitress said, in what was probably her usual annoyed voice.

"Both", the waitress and I said, simultaneously.

"What about toast?" She asked.

"Of course", I answered. "I almost forgot! Toast! We will have white toast, rye toast, whole wheat toast…"

"*Cinnamon* toast?" The waitress figured out the game by now.

"Yes, and an English Muffin".

"And for you, sir?"

"Oh, for me? Just coffee. I already had breakfast!"

Phyllis smirked as she slid her pencil back into the pocket of her apron. She reached out to retrieve our menus. Barbara still had hers in her hand and she wasn't letting it go. The waitress and Barbara played tug-of-war with her menu for a few seconds. Finally, Phyllis looked over to me. I motioned with my hand to let her keep the menu. Since we had nothing else to do until the food came, I figured this would be a good time to learn more about the most recent addition to my life.

"Barbara? Can you read?"

"A little", she answered, with her eyes still stuck on the menu.

I said, "What can you read on that menu?" Her eyes scanned back and forth.

"Hmm", she started, "two eggs…any st, st"

"Any style", I finished her thought.

"What does that mean?" Her little face looked up at me confused.

"Well", I answered, "do you remember when I ordered your eggs? Those were different styles of eggs. Some were scrambled, some were sunny-side up, like that".

Barbara's eyes worked their way back toward the kitchen. "So, you mean that they have all of those different kinds of eggs back there?"

I laughed a little, under my breath. "No, Sweetie. They only have one kind of egg back there. The cook just cooks them differently"

"Wow", she exclaimed, still looking toward the kitchen. "That cooker-guy must be pretty smart!"

"Yeah", I finished her thought. "Pretty smart".

Her eyes landed back on the menu. As I looked two tables over, I saw a family with two little kids, both who were busy coloring on placemats designed for kids with crayons. I caught Phyllis' eye and pointed at the kids then made a coloring motion with my hand. Phyllis nodded. A couple of seconds later, she placed a coloring page placemat in front of Barbara and dropped a box of crayons on the table. I gestured a thank you to Phyllis.

“Barbara, do you know what these are?” Her eyes lit up a little. It was very charming to see her even slightly happy. I made a mental note to try to light up her eyes as often as I could.

“Yes”, she answered. “These are crayons. Are they mine to keep ?”

“Sure, you can keep them”, I answered. With what this breakfast was going to cost me, I figured the least they could do was to give me a box of crayons. I was a little surprised that she would want to keep these cheap little crayons. “Would you like to color now?”

“Okay”, she responded by putting down the menu and opening the box of crayons pulling one out.

“What color is that crayon?” I asked, as I pushed the placemat closer to her.

“Blue”, she said as she started coloring a flower on the mat.

“What kinds of flowers are blue?” I was wondering how much she knew about the world.

“Blue flowers, I suppose”, she answered. That seemed like a pretty well-formed answer for a 5-year old. After all, I don’t know what kinds of flowers are blue either. “You are a good colorer”. I hope she didn’t know that there was no such word “colorer”. “Where did you learn how to color?”

“Dorothy”, she said, without looking up.

“Ahh, Dorothy”, I answered. “And how do you know Dorothy again?”

“The park”, she said, wiping her nose with her sleeve.

“So, Dorothy in the park taught you how to color, huh?”

“Yep!” Barbara was on to the red crayon. “Do you have any more questions you would like to ask me?”

“Umm”, I thought, “not for the moment”. There was a long silence. Eventually, I realized that there was canned music in the restaurant and I could hear that they were playing an excerpt from Mozart’s “The Magic Flute”. I thought it was time to interject a little culture into the conversation. “Hear that music?” Barbara didn’t even nod. “That was written by the greatest composer of all time: Wolfgang Amadeus Mozart. It is called *Die Zauberflöte* Kochel 620”. Barbara was unimpressed. Kochel is just a German word that means “Work”. But in English, the name of this opera is ‘the Magic Flute’. It is one of Mozart’s greatest pieces. He wrote it just months before he died”. Barbara’s eyes stayed transfixed on the placemat.

“Gloria Jean may die”, she said, without looking up. I stared at her, unable to speak for a little while. Finally, I grabbed her hand and stopped her from coloring.

“Barbara, who told you that?” She looked up slowly.

“She is in the hospital. You don’t go to the hospital unless you are real sick”. She looked back down at the placemat.

“Barbara, Gloria Jean isn’t going to die…well, she is going to die some day, but not for a long, long time”. I thought that maybe switching back to the music lesson would provide some levity into the morning. “Do you know any music?” I tried to change the subject as quickly as I could.

“Yes”. By now, her eyes were back on her coloring.

“What do you know about music?” I cracked a smile.

“I know a song”, she said, as she changed the blue crayon for the yellow one.

“What song do you know?” I seemed to hit on a topic a little closer to home for a 5-year old.

“Thistle Man. Dorothy taught it to us”, she said, as she changed crayons yet again.

“Ahh, Dorothy again. Would you like to sing your song?” I could barely wait to hear this.

“Okay”, she said.

Thistle Man
He played one
He played nick-nack on my thumb

“What?” I interrupted. “No, it is this *old* man!”

“Do you know that song, too?” Her face was off of the coloring placemat and her eyes lit up.

I started to answer, but my gaze was distracted by plates of food being set onto the table.

As the food was piled onto the table, Barbara’s eyes got bigger and bigger. At first, she didn’t think the food was for her, but the waitress kept pushing plate after plate under her nose.

“Try these”, I said, as I slid the plate of cinnamon toast under her massive eyes. She looked like a child on her first Christmas morning.

There was no way that anyone could have eaten as much food as I ordered, but Barbara dug in, trying a little bit of everything.

Her tiny little stomach seemed to bulge out of her blue jumper. Finally, she said:

"I can't eat any more". It was well past the time that I was supposed to be back at the office. As we were walking out she asked, half apologetically: "Do you think we could come back here again some day?'

"Sure we can", I answered. "We didn't have cereal!"

I hailed the first cab I could find, which wasn't that easy at 2:00 on a Monday. I hurriedly pushed Barbara in and climbed in behind her. Her eyes were getting heavy and she started to yawn. She was almost asleep, partially because it was so hot in the cab, but also because she was so full of pancakes. I thought to myself, "this is crazy! I can't do this. I don't know anything about raising children – and she's asleep". Within 4 blocks, her head was slumped over and she was out cold. I could feel that same "little devil" voice that I heard in the park, the one who told me to leave Barbara sitting on the swing in the park step up to the plate. It said,

"Dump her at the closest police station! She is asleep; she won't even know you are gone!" After all, I thought, I did my part; I fed her full of eggs. What Gloria Jean was asking for was unreasonable. It was time to let some trained professionals solve this problem". I said to the cab driver,

"I will bet you know the city pretty well?" He looked at me in the rear view mirror with a puzzled expression on his face.

"I have been driving this cab for 17 years, mister", he snorted. I know where just about everything is".

"Well", I started, "you see…I have this little problem…actually, it is not a problem per se…it is more like a recent turn of events…"

“Look, mister, I am a cab driver”, he belted back. “I don’t sell dope and I don’t hustle women. I drive people to where they want to go and they pay me. Are we clear about that?”

I figured I would quit beating around the bush.

“Do you know where the closest police station is”, I asked him. Startled, he looked at me in the rear view mirror.

“Police station? What do you want with a police station?” The veins were popping out of his neck.

“Well…this little girl…” I started to say. At that, I looked down at Barbara, who now was slumped over her with her tiny head against my arm. She looked helpless and vulnerable and alone. I was all she had. “Ah, nothing. Forget I brought it up”. Looking down and seeing her sleeping little face must have activated the “Dad” genes in me. There would be no dropping her off anywhere. She wasn’t going to a police station or anywhere else. She was *my* child and she was staying with *me.* I don’t know how this all happened…well, actually, I *do* know how it all happened – I got an old girlfriend pregnant, but I never thought that that would turn into this. Despite that, she was here and this was happening and I was in charge. It was time for me to quit trying to pawn this off onto someone else and to “cowboy up”. In that brief second, I went from feeling a huge burden being lifted off of me to being ashamed of myself for even thinking of such a thing. I figured the thing to do would be to scoop her up and put her on my lap. That thought made me even more nervous than asking Barbara if we could hold hands. I thought about it then decided not to, then I decided to do it again. I could hear my crazy Irish grandmother saying:

“If something seems like it’s the right thing to do, it usually is”.

I just about had myself talked into it. Looking at it logically, what would have been the worst that could happen? She could slap me? I have been slapped by bigger girls than her before. I slid my left hand behind her back and down her left leg and pulled her onto my chest. Her little body tensed up and she made a little frightened sound.

"Shh! It's okay, Sweetie. I've got you...you're with .....*your dad* now", I whispered, as I stroked the left side of her face with my right hand. Did I just say that? Did I just say, "you're with *your dad* now"? I guess so. I guess I was her dad. And, I guess I was acting like a dad would act. I could feel her face rest against my chest. I could feel her tiny little heart beating. Her hands were closed in fists, but as soon as she was in my lap, they opened, revealing sugar packets in each hand. In the folds of her jumper, there was dozens of packets of jelly. In between eating 15 pounds of breakfast food, this little thief somehow managed to steal everything in the place. I was half expecting to find the cook in there.

By the time I got back to the office, Toodles was furious.

Chapter 10
"Danny Introduces Buttercup to Toodles"

I walked into the office carrying Barbara, who was still sound asleep.

"Where have you been?" Toodles screamed. "You left here 2 hours ago, I have no idea where you are, you don't answer your cell phone and *now* you come back here with some dirty little girl!"

"I have a good idea", I said, under my voice, "Why don't you scream a little louder. Maybe *she* will wake up and *she* can fill you in on all of the details", I said, gesturing to Barbara. "Toodles..., *this* is what Gloria Jean called about. This is...well...my daughter!"

"I *know* who she is, Danny", Toodles said, interrupting me. "I sweat it out of Gloria Jean when I had her on the phone. I just didn't think it was gonna happen this quick."

"Take her to a conference room with a couch and make her a bed", I said, handing Barbara to Toodles. "She will wake up eventually. Have some crayons and colored paper for her to play with when she does. And *be nice* to her!"

"Oh, being nice to *her* will be no problem", Toodles ranted. "It is *you* that I would like to hit over the head!"

"And, one more thing, could you get my sister on the phone?", I said, as I walked toward my office.

"Which sister do mean, 'Daddy'?" Toodles answered sarcastically. "You have 5 of them!" Toodles was obviously steamed.

"The one that is the social worker, whichever one that is". I said as I closed my office door.

"That would be Moira" she said dismissively. Under her breath, she said, "He is going to try to raise a little girl and he can't even remember his sisters' names!" Toodles was beside herself with all of the recent developments.

About a minute later, the phone on my desk rang. Picking it up, I said:

"Moira?"

"Danny, what is going on? Toodles sounds like someone just repealed the slavery laws." My sister was in rare form.

"Which is *exactly* why I am calling you", I continued. "Hypothetically speaking, let's say that someone from my past claimed that she gave birth to a child and that I was the father of that child. Further, let's say that she told me she had to go into drug dependency clinic for a while and turned the child over to me...."

“Jesus, Mary and Joseph, Danny, what exactly is going on here?” Moira exploded.

“Remember, Gloria Jean?” I asked sheepishly. “Well…she called me today. I met her in the park….and…well…the long and short of it is, You are…an *Aunt*!”

“Danny, please tell me you are kidding! You have a kid?”

“No, Moira, I am not kidding, and yes, I have a kid. What do I do?”

“You have a child?”

“Yes, a little girl, named Barbara, but she likes to be called Buttercup”. I responded.

“Where is she now”? Asked Moira.

“Well…she is in a conference room…coloring, I assume. I put Toodles in charge!”

“She is *with* you…? *Now…*? Where is Gloria Jean” asked Moira in a heated tone.

“Where all drug offenders go, I guess. Off to the land of Methadonia. The bigger issue is what am I supposed to do with a 5 year old girl?”

“This explains why Toodles wants to kill you”, Moira screamed. “Well, the first thing you have to do is to be able to prove you have legal custody of her. If you can’t, you could get arrested for kidnapping”.

“Oh, believe me, I have already had that conversation with *several* people today. Will her birth certificate help?” I asked

"Only if you are named as the father". Moira replied.

"Well, the name on the birth certificate is Barbara Danielle McCullen".

Moira said, "Well, we have that going for us. How old is she?", she continued.

"It looks like she is 5". I stated.

"Well, you have to take her to a doctor and make sure she doesn't have any medical conditions", she said. Then we have to start making plans for school for her.

"School?" I was stunned at the weight of the situation. "Maybe dropping her off at that police station…" I kept myself from finishing that sentence.

"Danny, what did you just say?" Moira was steaming.

"Oh, nothing", I tried to slip in innocuously.

"Did I hear you right?", my sister continued. "Did you say that you were thinking about abandoning her at a police station?"

"No…well I did, but for a moment…a brief moment…I thought….but I quickly, *quickly* reconsidered".

"Well, good, Buddy", Moira continued. "Because if I ever…*ever*… hear you talk like that again, I will personally beat the crap out of you! When is Gloria Jean coming back?"

"It may be up to 3 months", I told her.

“Oh, Brother”, Moira answered, obviously reeling with this sudden turn of events. “This is gonna take a lot of work to pull this off, Danny!” Moira yelled.

“I am beginning to realize that”, I said, half to her and half to myself. “…Largely because she doesn’t seem to have any earthly possessions, other than the clothes she is wearing and a stuffed animal”.

“…And the hits just keep on rolling”, Moira continued. “Alright, here’s what we are gonna do. I will come over right after work. You and I can buy her some clothes and stuff. I will talk to her and see if I can sort all this out”.

“Yes, and we will probably have to burn the clothes she is wearing. The ones she is wearing are filthy!” I retorted. “She desperately needs a bath”.

“Danny, this is something that is vitally important. You can’t *give* her a bath”

“Moira, you have no idea how filthy this child is!”

“No, I mean, *you* can’t give her the bath. Danny, there are going to be eyes are on you. People are going to wonder how a 5 year-old girl just appeared in your life. It is going to be necessary for you to take a high road - on lots of things. You can’t be in the room when she is undressed. Not even for a minute! You can’t walk in on her while she is on the toilet or anything. She must have her own bedroom and she must *never* sleep in bed with you. If any of those things happen and somebody wants to make trouble for you, you could end up losing her forever and a case could easily be made that you are abusing her - and trust me, there aren’t too many thing that are worse than that”!

"Moira, three hours ago, I had a kid drop out of the sky and I am trying to do the right thing here and you and reading *me* the riot act…", I started to say, as my sister interrupted.

"Danny, I am deadly serious about that. Make sure none of those things ever happens!"

"You make it sound like I have some grand scheme in place…" I started, when again my sister interrupted.

"Danny, nobody said anything about any scheme, grand or otherwise. I am trying to help you here. Never, *ever* have any contact with that child when she is unclothed…*ever*!"

"Okay! You made your point", I interjected.

"I will see if I can find some daycare centers that she can go to until school starts. I will see you tonight", Moira said.

I hadn't even thought about that. I guess she can't sit in my office day and night. There were so many things that I had to do. It was as though a human appeared out of thin air, with nothing but the clothes on their back, and I had one day to put together a life for her; which is exactly what happened.

Chapter 11
"Planning for the Next 90 Days"

That night, Moira, Barbara and I went to every clothing store, every drug store and every toy store on earth. It got to the point that I just kept my credit card in my hand. We bought shirts and shorts and shoes and socks and underwear and toothbrushes. She wasn't that interested in toys, largely, I think because her mother probably told her she couldn't have them. I think she thought of them as a guilty pleasure, so she passed on most of the things that I picked out for her.

After our marathon-shopping spree, it was time for dinner.

"We don't have to eat pancakes again, do we?" Barbara said in her squeaky little voice.

"No, let's have hot dogs" I said. Every kid in America likes hot dogs, I thought.

"Barbara, why did you take all of the sugar packets with you from that restaurant this morning?" I asked.

"That way, we can have sugar later". She said.

"That's a bad sign", Moira said to me under her breath. "It indicates that she and her mother had been living pretty 'hand to mouth'".

When we got to my house, Moira took Barbara into the kitchen while I put her new clothes in one of the spare bedrooms. They talked for a long time. Moira had a much better rapport with her than I did. Maybe it was because she was a woman. Maybe it was because she was a social worker. The only thing that I could think of to talk to her about was football and old dead music composers and since the Mozart discussion got me nowhere, I decided there would be no point in bringing up wide receivers.

Moira ushered me into the dining room away from Barbara.

"She is a mess, Danny", Moira started. She has been living in an abandoned building with her drug-abusing mother. She has had almost no contact with children and even less with functioning adults, other than Gloria Jean, who was getting high most nights. She keeps talking about some lady named Dorothy, but I think she made her up. She is half terrified, half expecting that you will abandon, her too. She is scared out of her mind". Then she looked at me strangely. "What's all this about you holding hands with porcupines?"

"Ah, nothing", I answered. "It is just something I made up to get her to open up to me".

"Well, it worked", she said. "She likes you. In fact, she thinks she 'wished you up'. If this Dorothy lady is real, she taught them how to wish on a star and, well, she has been wishing for her father to enter the picture and whisk her away....and here you are! Now, she thinks you are Prince Charming!"

"Well", I answered, "That will be my aim!"

"That is the smallest part of this battle", Moira continued. "You will have some rocky roads ahead...but if anyone can do this, it's you".

"Me?" I blurted out.

"Sure", Moira said, as she smirked. "You always were good with the ladies! Bears, biting her toes all night", she said, as smirked again. "Raising a kid isn't that hard, Danny. It's mostly just common sense. Hell, you deal with people all day; she's a person – just a little bit shorter than the other ones you are used to dealing with! You're gonna do just fine", she said as she got up on her tip-toes and kissed me on the cheek. "I have to go now", Moira said. "I will keep my eyes open for daycare centers. "In the meantime, put our new friend in the *bath tub* – and *remember what I said...*" Her words trailed off and she headed for the door.

I thanked Moira for her monumental efforts, then walked Barbara to the bathroom. I showed her where the soap and shampoo was, got her a washcloth and a towel, got a new pair of pajamas for her and began filling up the tub with water. After the tub filled up, I said:

"Wash your hair with this stuff", I said, handing her a tube of shampoo. "Here is a cup you can fill up with water. Dump the water over your head to rinse it out. When you are done with your hair…wash…everything else. Then dry yourself off and put on your pajamas on and I will dry your hair with a hair dryer".

"Gloria Jean…Mommy always gave me my baths", she said, a little confused.

I didn't want to get into the whole "watchful eyes" business with her, so I just said, "You are a big girl, Barbara. I think you are big enough to give yourself your own baths". She seemed to like that the fact that I thought of her as a big girl.

Even though I wasn't going to be in the room with her, no one said I couldn't stand on the other side of the door. I could hear her splashing the water and her singing. After a few minutes, I said:

"Are you washing your hair?"

"No", she said in a firm voice. At least she was honest. There was a long silent pause.

"Barbara? Are you okay? What's happening?"

From the other side of the door I heard her say, "I am fine. What is all of this stuff do?"

A little puzzled, I answered, "All what stuff?"

"All this stuff under the sink". It was obvious she was out of the tub, exploring the bathroom.

"What are you doing…are you out of the bath tub?"

The voice from the other side of the door said, "No…well yes. What is all of this for"?

Exasperated, I said "Never mind what it does. Get back in the bath tub before you slip and fall…and get hurt…and catch your death…"

"Okay", the little voice answered.

"Start washing your hair", I answered.

I could hear the shampoo squirt out of the bottle.

"This stuff is gooey", she said in a whiney voice.

"Just rub it in your hair." I stated.

"Okay". After a few seconds, she let out a little scream, then a bigger one. Finally, she was screaming hysterically.

"Barbara, what is wrong?" I hollered from the other side of the door.

"My eyes!" She exploded. "My eyes are burning"

My initial reaction was to run into the room. Then I remembered my sister's warning.

"Rinse your eyes out with water!" I hollered.

"I can't. It hurts to do that!" She was obviously trying to get the shampoo out of her eyes with her hands and her hands still had shampoo on them. At that moment, I regretted not buying baby "no tears" shampoo. Rubbing her eyes was making matters worse.

"Pick up the glass and fill it with water and dump it on your head", I said in a panic.

"I can't see. My eyes are closed", she screamed.

"Honey, it is in front of you, to your left!" I tried to be as reassuring as I could.

"I found it". She seemed to be a little calmer.

I could hear water pour over her head, then the glass fell into the tub. It must have slipped out of her soapy hands. She must have picked it up because I could hear her filling it up with water and dumping water on her head over and over.

"That's better", she stated.

After a few more minutes, she pulled the plug from the bathtub and began to dry herself off. She finally came out in her pajamas with her wet hair.

"I like your bathtub! It's *fun*!", she stated with glee!

"It wasn't that much fun for *me*", I thought!

After I dried her hair, I showed her where my bedroom was and walked her to the closest bedroom to mine.

"This will be your bedroom. You will sleep in here", I said.

"Where are you going to be?" She seemed to be sizing up the situation.

"In there." I pointed to my bedroom. "Do you want me to leave your door open?"

"No…yes…I don't care. What if I have to go to the bathroom in the nighttime?" She was fidgeting with her stuffed dog.

"The bathroom…is where you took your bath". I guess the things that seemed obvious to me weren't so obvious to her. "Would you like me to leave the bathroom light on?" I was wondering if she was going to ask if she could sleep with me. I was glad she didn't.

"Okay!" She didn't seem to care one way or the other, but she had to answer something, and "okay" was as good to her as "no". We stood there looking at each other.

"Would…you like me to tuck you in?" It seemed like a fatherly thing to ask.

Her little face looked totally confused. "What does…."

"You mean…?" I stopped myself from finishing my own sentence. Of course no one ever tucked her in, she probably never slept in a real bed before. "C'mon", I said, as I reached out my hand. I was a little surprised that she took mine. When we got to the bed, I pulled back the covers and she crawled in. I pulled the blankets up to her chin. She pulled her arms out and put them over the covers. Her stuffed dog was in her right hand. Looking at the dog, she said.

"Murgatroid, this new bed sure is pretty soft, huh?" Her eyes shot up to me.

"Good night, Barbara".

"Have a nice sleep!" She shot a smile like I was taking her picture.

"Have…?" I never heard that before "Good night", I echoed. I stood up and started out of the room. When I reached the door, I heard her tiny voice behind me. It seemed a little panicked.

"Danny?" I had no idea what she wanted, or why she called me back, but her voice filled me with emotion. Without stopping, I turned one hundred and eighty degrees and walked back to her bed. When I got there, I put my left knee on the bed and crouched down over her. I put one hand on each side of her head and kissed her on the forehead. When I straightened up, her little face was beaming.

"This is gonna work", I said almost under my breath.

"What?" She looked happy but confused.

"Nothing", I said.

As I crawled into my bed, I could hear her talking to her stuffed animal and singing.

Finally it got quiet, maybe the first quiet moment since that afternoon. I assumed Barbara had fallen asleep. Suddenly, everything about my house and my bedroom and my life felt different. It was as though I suddenly woke up in the middle of someone else's life. It was like everything I knew was suddenly wrong, different. My newest catharsis was interrupted when I heard a little voice break the silence:

"Danny".

"What?", I answered.

"Are you still there?" Her voice was both resolute and unsure of herself at the same time.

"Yes, I am still here".

"Okay", she replied.

"Barbara, go to sleep!" I said, trying to be firm, yet nurturing.

"Okay", she repeated.

It was clear to me that I wasn't the only one that felt that thing were different. Her world has been turned upside down, too. The difference was, I was an adult, with the power to address and alter things. She was a 5 year-old child, who depended on other people for her well-being. Right now, she was depending on me. I was going to have to do my best to not let her down.

Chapter 11
"Buttercup Reflects"

SOO! Gloria Jean is gone. She had to go into a hospital. She might die. That would…be…okay, I guess. No, wait a minute, that's not nice! That wouldn't be okay. That is not the way a nice girl talks. It's just that…well…she makes me stand on a corner with her and makes it so I can't go to school. She makes me sleep in that old building with wood over where the windows are supposed to be. But I guess maybe it could be that maybe someone is mean to her, too so she can't do more fun and more better stuff for me.

It sure is weird being 5 years old. Yesterday, Gloria Jean and I were sitting on a swing, then we were crying, and then I guess I forgot about it, but I sort of remembered it so I got sad again, now I am at Danny's house and I have more food to eat than I have ever seen in my whole life and I get new clothes, lots of 'em and this comfortable bed to sleep in.

I sure hope Danny keeps being my father, or whatever he is. Heck, I just hope I get to sleep in this bed a little while longer. He came in to where my bed was gonna be and he tucked me in. That was nice. Nobody every done that afore. Well, acourse no one ever done that before. I never slept in no real bed afore. Ya know, I was thinking. Danny is sort of…well…handsome, I guess. I don't really usually think about stuff like that too much but I kind of like the way he looks. THEN…he started leaving. I thought I ought to say "thanks" or something, acause he did about a million nice things for me. He bought me so much food, I thought I would esplode or something. Then, he knew I didn't have no other clothes to wear, so he bought me a ton of new outfits, and now he is gonna let me sleep in this bed. I guess saying "thanks" is something a good girl would do or something. It is not like I have had so much practice at being a good girl or nothing. I usually don't get to hardly see nobody or hardly ever talk to nobody or nothing. But I kinda thought, if I did, maybe he would keep on doing nice things for me. But that's not really why, not really. I think I should have said "thanks" because he DID do a lot of nice things, not because if I did he would do more nice things for me. I wanted to say *something* but I couldn't think of what to say. SOO, I said the first thing that shot into my head. I said,

"Have a nice sleep". I never said that before! I don't even know what made me thing of that. I just said it.

I am pretty sure he was just gonna leave and go get in his bed, but I got sorta scared. I got scared that he was gonna leave and leave me and forget all about me and stop being my dad or whatever he is. I didn't even think about it or nothing, I just called out his name. Then, he real fast spun around and came back, and guess what? He came back in and he like hugged me. He brushed my bangs back and kissed me on my forehead. I loved that! I got this tingly feeling and felt like a million butterflies were inside me. I can't even imagine how great that made me feel.

Then he left. It got dark and real quiet. He was gonna go to sleep in his bed and I was gonna go to sleep in mine. But I sort of got nervous AGAIN. What if he was playing a trick on me and left? What if I never saw him again? What if he was gonna go try to find Gloria Jean and tell her he didn't want to be my dad anymore? I better check.

"Danny". I thought that no one would answer me. I heard his big-man voice say:

"What?" Maybe I should be glad he answered. He couldn't have answered if he left. I am so scared right now that I don't even know what I should do.

"Are you still there?" I asked that kinda quiet, but not too quiet.

That big man voice said something.

"Yes, I am still here". Well, that is good. I better say something again fast.

"Okay", I screamed. His big man voice said,

"Barbara, go to sleep". I was glad that he said that. Now, I am pretty sure I could go to sleep now.

Chapter 12
"Barbara Becomes Buttercup"

Even though I spent $400 on clothes and breakfast cereal the day before, there were still a million other things I had to do before Barbara would be settled in. For one, I had no idea what to do with her while I went to work. For the very immediate, I was left with no choice but to do the only thing I could do: take her to work with me.

My alarm clock went off at the regular time. I started into the shower, almost forgetting about the "bundle of joy" that changed my life yesterday. I figured I would wake her up, and then let her lay in her bed while I got ready. Then, I would get her ready, we would eat breakfast together and off to the office I would go with her in tow.

My first stop was to the bathroom, followed by a stop into her bedroom. The door to her room was closed. "That was funny", I thought, because I purposely left it open. I knocked, not knowing what sort of state I would find her in.

"Barbara? Barbara, honey, it is time to get up". There wasn't a sound. After a few seconds, I knocked again and opened the door slowly, poking my head around the door.

"Barbara, you have to get up now. We have to go see Toodles." As I peered around the corner, I could see that her bed was empty. I flung the door open. I ran over to the bed and began patted it down with my hands, hoping she was hiding under the blankets. I threw one blanket after another off of the mattress desperately. She was nowhere to be found. My heart was pounded. Had I imagined the entire incident? Had someone broke in during the night and took her? Did she get scared and left to go find her mother?

"Barbara? Barbara, where are you?" I looked under the bed. My calls turned into screams. In a panic, I began running around the room, screaming.

"Barbara? Barbara? Buttercup?..." Each scream got louder and more horrified.

At that, the closet door opened. I saw her tiny little body lying on the floor, with one hand on the doorknob, rubbing her eyes with the other.

"Is it time to get up?", her little voice repeated.

"Oh my God!" I ran to the closet and threw my arms around her up. She didn't seem afraid. She thought it was the most natural thing in the world.

"Buttercup, what are you doing in that closet?" I stated in disbelief.

"Sleeping. I wasn't doing anything bad. Do we get to have breakfast before we go?" Her little voice was still half asleep.

"Why are you in the closet? Why aren't you in your bed?" I must have sounded like a mad man.

"Gloria Jean always made me sleep in there. That way if they came, they wouldn't take me away".

"Take you away?" I shouted. "What are you talking about?" I said in an exasperated tone. "Who is going to come? No one…*no one* is *ever* going to take you away…! *ever*! Do you *understand*?"

"Okay", she said, as she nodded.

"You scared the…" I stopped short. Her shocked smile shot across her face.

"You almost said a 'swear', didn't you?" She was laughing.

"I was so scared", I exclaimed.

"I'm sorry". Her smile disappeared.

"Don't ever do that again". My voice was still trembling.

"Okay", she said, in a chipper voice.

"Sleep in your bed from now on", I stated.

"Okay", she smiled and nodded her head.

As we started walking toward the kitchen, I picked her up.

"Who is going to come and take you away?" I asked.

"I don't know, that is what Gloria Jean always told me", she said plaintively.

"Well, no one is coming and you scared me half out of my mind, so don't do that ever again". I tried to be stern, but it was no use. I stopped in the hall with her tiny little body in my arms and stared into her big brown eyes "No one…is *ever* going to take you away from me…Buttercup!"

I carried the pajama-clad Buttercup into the kitchen. I sat her down in one of the chairs and opened the freezer.

"They tell me these toaster waffles are pretty good", I told her. "Have you ever had them?" Buttercup just shook her head. "I bought Maple Syrup, but I got the small bottle. After it is gone, we can try another flavor. Maybe you will like something else better like…I don't know, maybe you will like blueberry or strawberry better". She had the same nondescript look on her face, probably because she had no idea what I was talking about. "Here is my suggestion", I continued, "when we go to restaurants…and I anticipate going to a *lot* of restaurants…try different flavors of syrup and…try to remember which flavor you like best. Then, I can get you the type you like…the best". Buttercup looked down at the empty table. While I waited for the waffle to pop up, I put a glass of milk on the table. "Here is another thing, let's have eggs tomorrow" I continued. "You may find that you like eggs *better* than pancakes *or* waffles", I went on. I poured her a glass of orange juice and put it down next to the glass of milk. She looked up at me after I put the second glass down. Her eyes were a little watery. I wondered if she was afraid or nervous because she thought she was getting yelled at for sleeping in the closet. "Personally", I said, "I don't like waffles *or* pancakes. I think it is the syrup part that I don't like". She had no idea what I meant. For that matter, I felt that I was just rambling. "Oh, and here is another thing. This morning, I gave you a glass of milk *and* a glass of orange juice". I sort of pointed to both of them as I said that. I felt sort of stupid doing it. It wasn't like she lived in a cave or anything. She must have known that there were two glasses in front of her and that one had milk in it and the other one had orange juice in it. "Personally, I don't care which one you have in the morning. Theoretically, they are both good for you, but you tell me which one you like best and that will be the one that I can give you to drink in the morning, okay?" Her eyes dropped back onto the table. By now, the waffles popped up from the toaster. I put them on a plate and put the syrup and the butter on the table. "Lots of people like butter on their waffles", I said. "Let me show you how to put the butter on". I scooped the knife into the butter and spread it around on the waffles. By now, it was obvious to me that I had been doing all of the talking, and Buttercup looked like she was going to start to cry. I figured it was time to quit talking about butter and start checking in with her. "Is…everything okay", I asked.

In a very weepy voice, she answered "Yes!"

"What's the matter", I asked. "Don't you like waffles?"

"Sure", she answered. "I guess I do", she answered. Her eyes were full of tears. "It's just…it's just…" She was having trouble completing her thoughts.

I sat down next to her and put my left hand on her shoulder. "What's wrong, Sweetie?"

"Gloria Jean…I usually don't…umm…." Her eyes darted back and forth from my left eye to my right eye.

"Sweetheart, it is okay", I told her. "You can tell me…anything! Is something wrong? Do you miss your mom?"

She turned her little face until she looking me in the eye. A tear rolled down her right cheek. "Well…see…I don't normally *get* any breakfast". She paused. "I never *got* to sleep in a big bed before". There was another long pause. I reached over and wiped the tear off of her cheek. "Where we sleep it's cold…and I don't *have* blankets. I guess…"

I looked at her with my best "dad" face I could muster up, "Barbara, remember those bad days? Well, they are *over!* Things are going to be *different* from now on! You are never going to *be* hungry again. You are never going to *be* cold again. You are not going to be dirty and you are not going to have to go around wearing the same clothes day after day anymore. That is the *end* of that…and I am here to see to it!" At that, Buttercup started to cry. She buried her head in my chest. I threw my other arm around her and stroked her hair with my right hand. "This might be the best thing that every happened", I said "for *both of us!"*

She sat back in her chair and sniffled a little. She looked up at me and smiled a sort of embarrassed smile. Finally, she looked back at the plate of waffles.

"I think I am done, okay", she asked.

"Okay", I told her. "Take your plate and put it in the sink. Rinse it off under the faucet like this". As I was saying this, I picked up her plate and rinsed it off. "When you are done with your breakfast, go in the bathroom and wash that *weepy* little face of yours off and brush your teeth!" I tried to make a joke out of our personal situation.

"Could…you…help me with that", her tiny little voice asked. She answered like she was still afraid that the trap door would open at any minute and she would fall out of this world. I am sure that part of her question was trying to determine what the protocol was for washing her face and brushing her teeth in my house. After all, she never did wash her face or brush her teeth in this strange new place before. For that matter, maybe she never washed her face or brushed her teeth anywhere before. We went to the sink and I got her a washcloth and a towel. While she was washing her face, I got the toothbrush out that I bought last night. As she started brushing her teeth, she occasionally looked at my reflection for approval.

While she finished brushing her teeth, I went into her bedroom and laid out some clothes for her on her bed that was still devoid of blankets. I laid out a pair of pink overalls and a pink striped top. I had never picked out little girl's clothes before, so I guess I was going for the quintessential little girl look.

"Go change into the clothes I put out for you and we will get going, okay?" At that, she scampered down the hall and slammed the bedroom door. 5 minutes later, we were ready to leave.

Chapter 11
"Danny and Buttercup Show up at the Office"

When we got the office, Toodles was waiting.

"Well, Little Lady, don't you look *fine*, now that you are all cleaned up", she said, half sweetly, half condescendingly. Without even taking a breath, she looked at me with her teeth clenched and said:

"What is *she* doing here?" she said, as she walked me a few steps away from Buttercup.

"Well, what did you *think* I was going to do with her? Leave her at my house alone"? I tried to state my answer under my breath as much as I could. "I was hoping…"

"…That I would watch her?" Toodles finished my sentence.

"*While* you were looking for a daycare center". I said sheepishly.

"Like I have time to watch *her*, look for a daycare center for *her* and take care of *everything* else that happens around her?" Toodles said, in less than happy words.

"Well, look at the bright side! As soon as you find a daycare center that will take her, the faster things will be back to normal". I giggled awkwardly. "I guess I will have to tell Buttercup what's about to happen", I said, half to myself, half to Toodles.

“Oh, so now she is ‘*Buttercup’*, huh?”, said Toodles, in her condescending way.

“Well, yes. We had a ‘moment’ this morning”, I started to explain it, but realized that it was probably best left unspoken.

“I guess I will have to tell her that she can stay here today, but that we would look for daycare centers”, I said. I took Buttercup’s hand and started walking her into my office.

“And while you are doing it, *fix* that child’s appearance! She still has *tags* on her clothes”, said Toodles, as she walked toward her desk and picked up the phone.

My eyes dropped down to the hip of Buttercup’s overalls, to see a “Size 5” label. I quickly ripped it off and smiled weakly back at Toodles as I walked her into my office.

“Buttercup”, I started, “you can stay here today and maybe tomorrow, but Toodles and I…well more Toodles *than* I…will be looking for a daycare center for you to go to while I am at work.”

She looked down at her shoes. “So you mean…you are going to send me away?” she said in a thin, whiney voice.

“*NO*”, I nervously blurted out. “I am not sending you away …it is just while I am at work. You can go to….well…like to school! There will be other children for you to play with”, I tried to explain. “This is no place for you. You would have nothing to do all day”. I tried my best to explain the situation.

“What if you don’t come back?” Fear shot across her face. I just realized what was happening. She was abandoned by her mother, the only human she had ever known in her life yesterday and one day later, I was telling her I was looking for somewhere to send her.

"No, it is not like that! I will drop you off…at school…every morning. You will play games, have snacks, take naps there and I will come back and get you every night – *every night*". I had no idea what really happened at daycare centers. It was my best recollection of Kindergarten from years ago.

"Do you promise?" Her eyes got watery. Her lower lip quivered.

"Do I promise what?" If I were going to be making a promise, I felt I wanted to know what I was promising *to*.

"Do you promise you'll come back for me?" Her voice got tinier with ever word.

"I cross my heart and hope to *die* promise", I said, as I made a cross over my heart with my right hand. I decided to resist the urge to elaborate any more, as I am so wrought to do. Buttercup seemed a little relieved.

With her usual lightning precision, Toodles had found a daycare center that was 3 blocks away. She obtained all of the necessary paperwork, completed the paperwork and faxed it all back to them before lunch.

"They want to know what her Social Security Number is", she stated.

"I am not sure if she has one", was my retort. "How do you get a Social Security Number?" Before I could finish the sentence, Toodles was handing me the form.

At lunchtime, Buttercup and I walked three blocks to the daycare center. On the way, we stopped and got a pretzel from the vendor who had a rolling cart on the sidewalk. She ripped it in half and put the other half in her pocket.

"Who's the other half for?", I asked.

She shrugged as she looked at the sidewalk.

The daycare center was bright and colorful and had kids and toys and books and games everywhere.

"Hello, you must be Mr. Cullen", a woman with a confident smile said. "And this must be Barbara", she said, as she eyed Buttercup. "I am Lynn Johnson, the director here". Her speech was highly practiced. With what daycare would be costing me, she should be at least that cordial.

"She likes being called 'Buttercup'", I said.

"Well, then Buttercup it is", her smile got bigger. "I understand you may be joining us soon", her bright institutional smile continued.

"*Very* soon", I chimed in. "Maybe she could look around for a little while today and then come back for a full day soon", I added.

Miss Johnson said, "that would be a wonderful idea!"

Buttercup stood there, in front of 20 kids, all running around playing with a million toys still holding my hand. Eventually, I let her hand go. She looked up at me and then back at the kids. It was obvious she had never seen anything like this before. She began to walk toward the toys and other kids. She looked back at me. I gave her a reassuring look. She looked as though she was going to run back to me, but the temptation of every toy on earth was too much for her to resist. I sat on the floor with my legs crossed and watched her explore the room filled with a myriad of games and puzzles.

After about an hour of her awkwardly interfacing with kids, some her own age, some not, I said "Honey, we have to go, now!"

She walked back over. Facing her, I took one of her hands in each one of mine.

"Can I come back tomorrow", she asked, looking at the floor.

"Yes you can", I stated. Mission accomplished, I thought to myself.

Chapter 11
"Wednesday"

It was all arranged. I would take Buttercup to the daycare center, go back at lunch time, eat lunch with her, pick her up at 4:30, and take her back to the office until it was time for us to go home. I could see how my career path would need some serious modifications. Client lunches and dinners would need to be cancelled. So were late nights at the office.

The next day, we got to the daycare center at 8:00. , I hugged Buttercup outside the playroom and said:

"Okay, sweetie. I will see you at lunch-time".

She pulled back from my embrace and looked me straight in the eyes.

"Promise?" Her voice was so fragile that it almost broke my heart. She crossed my heart with her finger.

"I *promise!"* I smiled as I made a cross over her heart. Then, I pulled her tight to me once more.

At that, she ran away to get lost in the sea of kids.

Chapter 12
"Trouble a'brewing"

Other than the fact that my sales numbers were extremely off, and I wasn't spending anywhere near as much time at the office as I once had, Buttercup and I were working out just fine. Every morning, I made her breakfast, got her dressed and took her to daycare. Every afternoon, I went back to the daycare center, ate some weird bologna sandwich or peanut butter and jelly sandwich with her and every night, I picked her up, and took her back to the office, where she would hang around for an hour or two sitting at the conference table in my office, drawing pictures, and finally back home. One night, I caught her staring at something out the window and mumbling.

"Who are you talking to?" My words snapped her back to reality

"No one…nothing", She mumbled half to herself and half to me. "I guess I don't have to do that anymore". She looked at me and then jumped down off of the window sill. "Dorothy was right", she said, as she jumped down.

"Right about what?", I followed up.

"Oh, you know", she said, "just about stuff". Her words seemed to drift off. Maybe some day I would understand what that all meant, but for now, it was going to have to remain one of life's mysteries. At that, she ran down the empty hall in my office building. She liked to "explore" the adjacent offices, and conference rooms. She would take her stuffed dog Murgatroid with her and pretend she was walking him. She liked to color and found great joy in decorating every square inch of wall space she could find, both at home and my office with pictures. Some of the other sales people would see me in the hallways and would say,

"Tell Buttercup 'thanks' for the drawings".

I would apologize for her invading their offices. No one ever seemed to mind. The proud GLG staff began to think of her as not "my kid", but as "our kid". My fellow co-workers would bring in clothes that didn't fit their kids anymore and give them to me for Buttercup. It got to the point that people would see me without her, and they would and say:

"Where's Buttercup?" Some of them didn't even know my name. I would respond by saying:

"She has to go to school *sometime",* and smile.

Toys and candy would show up on my desk with notes on them saying "Please give this to Buttercup". As she and I would leave the office at the end of the day, always hand in hand, people in the elevator would say:

"Bye-bye, Buttercup". Then, they would look at me. They would be embarrassed that they did not know my name, which made them blurt out a "...goodbye...!"

The impossible was happening. A five year old, brown eyed little girl was forcing a cold, heartless investment planning firm into growing a heart.

Around the middle of the third week, Toodles took a call from Lynn Johnson.

"She wants to meet with you when you pick up Buttercup tonight", Toodles said, speaking of Lynn Johnson.

"Great" I responded. "I am a father for two weeks and already a 'parent-teacher' conference".

When I got to the daycare center, I instinctively went straight to the 5 year old room. Ms. Johnson was waiting for me there.

"Mr. Cullen, is this a good time for us to talk?" It was the first time I didn't see the institutional smile painted on her face.

"Sure, let me just get Buttercup…" I started to say. At that, Buttercup saw me and ran over next to my side.

"Perhaps, she should stay here while we meet alone", she said in a serious voice.

Looking down at Buttercup, I said "I'll be right back, Honey".

Without saying a word, her lips mouthed out "Promise?" She crossed her heart with her finger.

Smiling, I looked down and mouthed out "Promise". I made a cross over my heart.

Buttercup was conflicted, and who could blame her? At this point, anything that veered off of our normal routine was bad, as far as she was concerned. It was the best I could do to assure her that I would be *right* back.

Ms. Johnson led me to her office. It had a desk near the windows with chairs in front of it, obviously set up so she could meet with parents.

"Mr. Cullen", she began to say, "Buttercup is a charming little girl". She said that like she had another shoe to drop. "But I think we will have to sever our relationship with you and her".

"What is it?" I asked. "The checks haven't bounced, have they?" I said that as snidely as I could.

"Oh, no, it is not that at all" she said, almost apologetically. "Let me start at the beginning", she continued. "For starters, she is cognitively behind most of the other children in her group".

"Ms. Johnson, my sister is a Social Worker. She told me to expect that", I explained. "Her home life before she came to live with me was tumultuous". I figured there was no point in telling her that she used to live with her 'bag lady' mother in God-knows what kind of home-life. "She told me that within 3 to 6 months, her cognitive skills should match children her age", I continued.

"That is not all", Ms. Johnson continued. "She has a hard time socializing with other children", Ms. Johnson went on.

"Again", I interjected, "I think that this is the product of her rocky background. My sister feels that with a little time and stability, she will look and act like every other child!"

"Well, that is fine, Mr. Cullen, but there is one more thing…She steals!" Ms. Johnson stated that almost as through she was ashamed of herself for having to say it.

"She what?", I said, in a disbelieving voice.

"Things have been turning up missing ever since she got here", Ms. Johnson was certainly uncomfortable with this conversation. "Not only have things of the school's been disappearing, but mothers have reported that the other children are missing toys and personal effects from their cubbies and their lunch boxes".

There was a long silence. "What makes you think it is Buttercup that has been taking these things?" I asked in an accusatorial voice.

"Because….we have found them with her. She takes things and hides them and retrieves them later. I found Brittany Reilly's toy pelican stuffed in Buttercup's pant leg". Ms. Johnson was deeply embarrassed by her statement.

"Do you mind if I talk to her privately about this?" I asked. "Can you set your judgment aside until I have an opportunity to deal with this?"

"Certainly, but we will have to see a radical and rapid change", Ms. Johnson said.

"May I use your office?" I asked.

"Certainly", Ms. Johnson said. "If you like, I can get her now!"

A few minutes later, Ms. Johnson reappeared at the door holding Buttercup's hand.

"Hi Danny!", she said, with delight.

"Honey, can we talk about something?" I said matter-of-factly.

"Okay". Her face looked like someone who was about to be in trouble.

"I will leave you two alone", Ms. Johnson said, as she closed the door.

Buttercup walked slowly toward me. I picked her up and put her on my knee.

"Honey, Ms. Johnson is mad at you", I said.

"I'm sorry", her little voice answered. She was so willing to please that she apologized before she even knew what Ms. Johnson was mad at her for.

"Honey, Ms. Johnson tells me that you have been stealing", I explained. "Do you know what that means?", I asked.

"No". Buttercup looked at her shoes, which is what she did when she didn't know what was going to happen next.

"She said you have been taking things that don't belong to you", I explained. "Is that true?" I questioned.

"Well…only sometimes", she whispered, still looking at her shoes.

"Honey, why would you do that?" I asked, trying to make sense of it.

"I don't know", she answered.

"No, I am sorry, 'I don't know' is not going to cut it this time. Why do you take other children's' things?" I asked.

"Because….they have nice things…and I don't. I just wanted to…". Her little face stuttered and stammered to try to spit out the story. After those few short words, I understood. It was time to let her up off the mat.

"You wanted the same toys and things that the other kids have?" I asked.

"Yes. Are you mad at me, too now? Are you going to send me away…to the place?" She put her head against my chest.

"No…I am not going to *send* you anywhere. Why didn't you just *tell* me you wanted more toys? My God, Buttercup, you can have anything you want." I said that as much to reassure myself and I did to make her understand.

"But…toys cost money…and we don't have any money". Buttercup was obviously reliving a sermon she heard from her mother many times before.

It was starting to sink in. The packets of sugar in her sleeping hand. The jelly crammed into the hem of her filthy jumper. The half of the pretzel in her pocket. These were the self-defense mechanisms she taught herself to survive in the strange world she was forced to become accustomed to.

"Let's make a deal", I said. "We will go shopping for toys this weekend. We will get you some toys and those toys will be yours. No one will have the right to take them away from you, not me or anyone else. But in exchange for that, you have to promise not to take things that are the property of other children. You can play with them, if it is alright with the children, but when you are through or when they ask, you have to give them back. Is it a deal?"

I felt like it was up to me to try to explain the world and all of its inner workings to this child, as if she has been raised on a distant planet.

"Okay". She seemed comfortable with that arrangement. "Will Ms. Johnson stop being mad at me?"

"I hope so", I added.

When I opened the door, Ms. Johnson was on the other side.

"May I have a word with you, Ms. Johnson?"

"Certainly, you may", Ms. Johnson responded.

Without getting into too many graphic details, I explained how Buttercup was raised by her indigent mother who was doing the best she could to keep herself alive. I explained that Buttercup felt the only way she would ever get to have what every other child in the daycare center had was to steal them. I also told her about the arrangement Buttercup and I struck and that the thievery should stop.

"Based on that, I would like to ask you for another chance", I told Ms. Johnson.
"If I have learned anything about my daughter in the last few weeks, it is that if Buttercup says she is going to do something, she is as good as her word", I stated. "largely because she is still not totally convinced that I am not going to abandon her...which I have *no* intention of doing", I hurriedly added.

"Well, based on those circumstances, I see no reason not to give her another chance", Ms. Johnson added. "After all, she has gone through a maelstrom of change during the last several weeks as it is, the last thing she needs is one more". Ms. Johnson felt resolute about her decision.

The current crisis seemed to be solved.

Chapter 13
"The Calm – followed by The Storm"

Days turned into weeks. Buttercup seemed to be turning into a normally adjusted child, with toys she liked to play with and favorite foods she liked to eat. She loved having me read to hear while she sat on my lap. Most nights would find us with her on my lap on the couch, under a blanket, watching something on Television. It didn't seem to matter to her what I was reading or what we were watching. I think she just found great comfort in being close to me. No longer would I find food hidden in her clothes or in corners of her bedroom. The thievery stopped. She did play with some of the kids in the neighborhood, but she always turned down offers for sleep-overs. I think she was afraid that if she slept anywhere but in her own bed, that she would never get to come back to our house - her house. The things that used to be a chore at first, became welcome additions to my day. I missed her when she was not around. I missed her tiny voice asking me why some flowers were blue and some were red. I missed her soft, brown eyes. I could sit with her in my lap all day long. I was happiest man in the world when she would crawl into my lap and fall asleep. Photographs of her surrounded my desk. I showed her pictures to strangers in the elevator. She seemed to be loving her new life, too. One night, we were sitting on the couch watching some kid show on DVD, as usual. She was sitting on my lap and both of us were wrapped up in a blanket. I had seen the DVD so many times, I knew it by heart. In one part, there was a long silence. As the lights from the TV flashed on her face, she turned her head and stared at me. Finally, I heard her little voice say:

"Danny…I love this!" Her words were so simple, yet so full of meaning. I was waiting for her to say, "I love this part" or "I love this story". She didn't. She seemed be saying that she loved this new life. She was safe and sound and warm and full of food and being nurtured…and happy. And I was happy, too, for the first time….maybe, ever. I was so choked up, I couldn't speak. I bent down at the neck and kissed her on the left temple. The lights of the television continued to flash on her face. 5 minutes later, she was sound asleep.

My sales, which were once in the top 5 of the firm, suffered significantly. No longer was I the "big-shooter" in the office. Gone were the days of being the first to arrive and the last to leave. Power-lunches were replaced with Peanut Butter and Jelly sandwiches. I still made a comfortable living, but it was nothing like what I had been making. The money didn't matter to me, one way or the other. It never mattered to me in the first place. What did matter, about the only thing that did, was that I had my little girl in my life.

Chuck Patterson, my boss was a serious man. He would "interface" with me regularly, stating that "these times", meaning this robust economy, I guess, wouldn't always be here, and I should prepare for them now. He didn't care about me or my ability to support myself when the economy turned south, all he cared about was his quota for this month, which he, without my Herculean efforts, was not attaining.

One gray Wednesday, everything that was good, started to erode. Toodles knocked on my office door, opened it, and stuck her head into the room with a worried look on her face.

"Mr. Cullen, these men have some papers they want you to sign".

Toodles never called me "Mr. Cullen", unless there was a huge client present or unless there was trouble. It was the latter.

"Well, let them in", I said.

The two men in dark suits, with serious looks on their faces handed me a wad of papers. They waited briefly while I tried to read them.

"Mr. Cullen, we know you are a busy man. If you just sign at the bottom, we won't need to trouble you anymore", the taller man said.

"Sir, I haven't even read them yet", I snapped.

"Perhaps I can shorten the process and assist you toward bringing this matter to a close. We are here to see that Barbara Danielle McCullen is returned to her biological mother forthwith and that you relinquish any parental or residential obligations in or around this infant child", he said, in a clinical voice.

"Excuse me, but the last I knew, Barbara's mother was addicted to an illegal chemical substance and was indigent. She was not able to support herself, much less care for an 'infant' child". I said "infant" with all of the disrespect I could. I knew that in the eyes of the law, everyone is considered an "infant" until they reached the age of 21.

"Things do change, Mr. Cullen. Gloria Jean Novak has been released from the Chemical Dependency Unit and is currently in the care of the state. She is living in a half-way house and is interested in returning to a normal life as soon as possible. This includes caring for her minor daughter". His words were carefully chosen, as though these were thoughts that he had delivered hundreds of times before.

"Lest we not forget that the last time I saw 'Ms. Novak', she did willfully and without reservation, turn over said minor child to me, the child's *biological* father. Seeing as how she didn't have the financial resources or the 'any-other' resources to care for her child – *our* child – *my child*, she *voluntarily* turned her over to me!" I was glad I took that Business Law class in college. It prepared me for making stupid statements like "…turn over 'said' child".

"The terms of that meeting and your legal standings in regards to harboring said minor child, are not only the subject for a court to decide, but are widely contested", he furthered.

"What does that mean? Is she saying…? What is she saying? What are you trying to imply…?" I said in a highly accusatorial manner.

"Mr. Cullen, I am not her to 'imply' anything. And I am certainly not here to attempt to evoke any unwanted emotions in you…" he started to say.

"Well, then you have failed miserably", I screamed, jumping to my feet. "Is she saying that I kidnapped Buttercup? The only thing that is more ridiculous than that is the fact that you believe her!" My tone was inflamed. "If you think you can waltz in here with a piece of paper from a state agency and take '*my daughter'* away from the only safe, nurturing environment she has ever known, one where she doesn't have to sleep in the closet of an abandoned buildings to avoid being abducted or taken away from her mother, then you are wholly mistaken!" I think everyone on the floor of my building heard this diatribe, both for the gravitas, as well as the sheer volume. Looking past them into the hall, I said:

"Miss Harrison, could you please see that our visitors' parking is validated". I stared at the taller one who did all of the talking. "There are *leaving",* I continued. Toodles knew only too well what was going on and didn't have to be summoned. She was only a step behind my words anyway.

"I can show you gentlemen the way out", Toodles exclaimed, harboring the same disrespect that I had.

"Then you can be assured that you will be arrested by the end of the day and forced to produce said infant child", my graven friend belted out, just before he turned and walked out of the office. He almost knocked Toodles over as he passed her at the door.

"Toodles, come in here", I beckoned. With my palms still sweating and with adrenaline pounding in my head, I grabbed a piece of stationary and a pen and wrote, "I Daniel P. Cullen do hereby grant power of attorney to Towanda Harrison, in any and all matters concerning the health and welfare of the minor child 'Barbara Danielle McCullen'".

"Sign this", I said. "Take it to someone, somewhere in this building and have it notarized. If I get arrested, you get Buttercup", I exclaimed, like a man whose life was flashing before his eyes.

"No problem", Toodles snapped, without hesitation.

As I rounded the desk, Toodles said:

"Where are you going?"

"To Legal", I retorted. "There are so many lawyers in this building, for the first 3 months I worked here, I thought everyone's last name was 'Esquire'", I explained.

I golfed with Sam Culbertson sometimes. He, like me, was not a blue blood, but in his case, it was no secret. He went to college on student loans and got a job as a police officer. At nights, he went to law school. I would learn over my long hours with Sam that his last name was changed from Cadogan, and old Gaelic name and that his grandfather was born in County Wicklow, Ireland. Sam's grandfather changed his name once he got to America because he thought that his "Irish-ness" would be a hindrance in getting a job. His story sounded familiar.

"Sam, I have a problem", I bellowed.

"Danny, everyone in this building could pretty much tell that" he stated in a calming voice. "Let's see what they served you with".

I didn't even realize it, but I inadvertently picked up the papers that "gray suit" plopped on my desk and was waving them around in the air.

He sat down at his desk with me sitting across from him. He picked up his reading glasses and began poring through the paperwork.

After several minutes, he said:

"Well, I will give it to those state agencies, they can write a pretty compelling summons", he said, as he removed his glasses. He began reaching for paperwork in his desk.

"Then they can just walk in here and take my daughter away just like that?" My tone replicated the one that I used to Mr. Gray Suit.

"Well, they can try", Sam said, in a calming voice. "Whether they can or not, is not the issue; they *aren't* ; not in this lifetime they aren't". Sam's distinction was lost on me. "They can generate paperwork, but let them see how *we* generate paperwork, *downtown"* Sam snorted. He reached over and hit the Intercom Button on his phone.

"Maysie, get Whittiker and Bradford in here, *now*", he said into the phone. "Danny, come back in an hour". He continued to thumb through paperwork as I got up to leave his office.

"Can you…" I started to say.

"Come back in an hour", Sam said reassuringly.

When I got back to my office, Toodles was waiting.

"What's going on?", she asked in a panicked state.

"I left it with Sam", I said. He told me to come back in an hour. What do I have next?" I asked.

"Next?" Toodles looked at me with amazement. She completely forgot we were there to buy and sell stocks and bonds.

"Oh, yes", Toodles continued, "the people from Johnson Hewell will be here at 3:00", she finished.

"Am I in the clear for a while?" I asked.

"Well, your call sheet has about 100 calls on it, but nothing that can't wait for a while", she retorted.

"Fine, I will be back in a half hour".

On the way to the elevator, Chuck Patterson, my boss stopped me.

“Hey, Danny, I was just getting ready to come and see you. Is this a good time for a chat?” He had his usual ‘serious’ expression plastered on his face.

“Actually, it isn’t, Chuck. I am on my way to a client meeting”. About the last thing I was in the mood for was one of Chuck’s “keep your nose to the grindstone” speeches. “I will get back to you be the end of the week”, I said and I kept walking.

I walked out of the door and into the street where I hailed a cab. All the while I was on the way to the daycare center, I assumed that a squad car would be pulling us over and arresting me for whatever the state decided it was that I was guilty of.

When I got to the daycare center, I walked in a hurried fashion. Ms. Johnson passed me in the hall.

“Mr. Cullen”, she said in a startled voice, “we don’t usually see you in the middle of the day”, said Ms. Johnson.

“I happened to be in the neighborhood”, I smiled, awkwardly.

“Is everything alright?” she followed up.

“Actually, I was getting ready to ask you that same question”, I responded. There was a long, gaping silence. “Buttercup seemed like she was catching a cold, this morning”. I made up a silly excuse to cover for my awkward behavior.

“I am sorry to hear that. She seems alright this morning”, reported Ms. Johnson. “I will ask her teacher to keep an eye on her, though”.

“Ms. Johnson, has there been anyone here today asking about her?” My statement certainly took Ms. Johnson by surprise.

“Why, no, this has been an extremely normal day”, she confined.

“Just so I know, what *would* happen if someone came here and told you to turn Buttercup over to them?” My question was followed up by an even longer pause.

“Unless we had a statement of compliance from you in our files, we wouldn’t even tell them she was here”. Ms. Johnson looked dumbfounded. “Mr. Cullen, are you sure that everything is alright?” She expressed genuine concern.

“And if they insisted?” I continued. “What if they had paperwork from…oh, let’s say the state demanding that she be released to them?” My tone grew more insistent.

“We would order an immediate lock-down of the daycare center and summon our lawyers here immediately. No one would leave here with her until it was determined that any party with any paperwork had the legal authority to do so. Mr. Cullen, are you sure there isn’t something you would like to tell me?” Ms. Johnson used the same clinical tone in her voice as she did with every other statement she made.

“No! Just ‘new dad jitters’ is all!” I said, trying to wave it off as though it were nothing.

I watched Buttercup run around the daycare center through the full-length glass windows. I didn’t want to walk in and get her as nervous as I have managed to get everyone else within a 2 square mile radius of me. I got a lump in my throat thinking that this might be the last time I may ever see her. I desperately wanted to run into the play room and wrap her in my arms and kiss her tiny little forehead, but I resisted the urge. It was better for her not to see me in such a panicked state anyway.

When I got back to the office, Toodles was practically waiting for me at the elevator.

"Danny, Legal wants to see you as soon as you get in. I cancelled all of your appointments for the rest of the day. I told everyone you were sick". As I started walking down the corridor, I noticed that Toodles was walking directly next to me.

"Where are *you* going?" I asked her.

"*I* am going with *you"* Toodles insisted. "If they think they are carting that little girl out of her, they will have to do it over my cold, dead body", she snapped.

When I walked into the legal wing, the secretary said, "They are waiting for you in the conference room, Mr. Cullen". The conference room was a little larger than most, but was filled up mostly with a rectangular table with seating for about 20 people. Twelve of the orneriest looking lawyers I had ever seen were all standing around one end of the table, each with they own stack of papers. There were women and men in that room that I have never seen before. They all expressed sentiments like "we are going to fight this, Danny", and "they will wish they never took this case on".

Sam made his way through the crowd. He said:

"Danny, we have enough paper work here to keep the state busy for awhile. We will file an immediate restraining order, demanding that Butter – ah 'Barbara' be domiciled with her father. That means she stays with you. We will bring Gloria Jean's sanity into question, for being admitted into a chemical dependency unit. Then, we will bring Gloria's *character* into question for abandoning her in the first place. We will argue that she is not fit to care for a minor child. You need to sign here, here, here, here and here". Sam rang through this with military precision.

"Should I read any of this first?" I quipped.

"*You* should *trust* us! We are due in court in 45 minutes!" Sam couldn't be more serious.

"Court? We are going to court?" I was flabbergasted.

"No, *you* are not going to court", Sam retorted. "If you show up, some overzealous Assistant District Attorney might arrest you. Then, we would have to draft another mountain of paperwork to get you out of jail. *You* are going to go pick up Buttercup, go home and not answer the door for anyone, not even the pizza delivery man. If we need to contact you, I will call you on my personal cell phone. If you don't see *my* name on *your* Caller I.D., don't answer it".

Even as Sam was giving me my instructions, he was ushering a clerk out of the door, along with me, sending him in one direction and me in another.

"Sam, how can I pay for all of this?" There was amazement in my voice.

"Pay? For what, Danny?" An odd look struck across his face. "Nothing happened here….right? At that, he turned around and looked garden-hose style at the roomful of lawyers. Every head nodded up and down with a look of how everyone would swear that I didn't just use thousands of dollars of GLG's money to prepare legal briefs for my personal matter. "We are a *family* here, Danny" Sam said. "Families go the matt for one another!" At that, Sam pushed me out the door.

Who could have imagined what this day would have brought? When I woke up this morning, it just seemed like another gray Wednesday. Yet, before 2:00 O'clock, I would be bullied by Child and Welfare agents and would put the law division of one of the biggest investment firms in the United States at my defense table. And the day was not over. A clerk was still going to file paperwork and I was going to pick up my daughter and go into hiding. For a moment, I was about to say, "Why me?" Then I remembered one of my grandmother's old sayings: "We don't ask 'why me' when the good things happen, why ask now". I certainly didn't spend much time *thanking* God for bringing Buttercup to me in the first place; why should I blame Him for potentially having to give her back? Sometimes, Irish common sense is the best.

Buttercup was both happy and confused to see me so early in the day. They were playing "Duck, Duck, Goose" when I walked into the playroom. She was running around the circle of children when she spotted me and ran toward me and jumped into my arms.

"Hello!" She exclaimed, with a bright smile on her face. "Is it 4:30 already?" she asked.

"No, I have a headache, so I decided we should go home early", I said as I picked her up. It was the best lie I could come up with on such short notice.

"I'm sorry", she said. "Would you like it if I rubbed your forehead?" Her tiny voice melted my heart.

"I would *love* that, Buttercup!" I bit back tears and she waved her little fingers across my face.

In the cab on the way home she said.

"How is your headache?"

"It seems to be going away" I said.

"When we get home, can you help me with a contest we are having at school? She asked.

"Sure", I answered, "What contest?"

"We are supposed to write an essay…what's an essay?" Her inquisitive voice went on.

"Well, it is like a story, I answered. "What kind of story is it? What are you writing about?" I asked.

"Well, we get to pick", she said. "We can either write an essay about how much we love our mom or our dad. Can it be about you?", she said.

"Of course it can", I answered.

"Danny…do you love me?" Her voice got smaller with each word.

"Sweetheart, I love you to death", I replied.

"Danny…would you ever slap me?"

"Slap you?" I couldn't believe she would ask such a question. My first response was to remind her that I had hardly ever even scolded her, much let strike her.

"Sweetheart, there is no way that I will *ever* slap you", I said. "What's more, if anyone else ever slapped you, they better start running, because I would be right behind them. If I ever caught them, I would murder them". After I said that, I got nervous. Did someone, somehow get to her and tell her to say that I was abusing her? Worse, was she trying to tell me that someone at the daycare center *was* abusing her?

"Would you slap me…if I called you…'daddy'". There was a long hideous silence. "The other girls call their fathers 'daddy'", her little voice went on. "I would like to do that, too". Her voice got tremendously soft. "Would that be okay? Would I get slapped if…?" Her voice trailed off.

As I looked down at the tiny little angel who sat next to me, I could hardly talk for the lump in my throat must have been the size of a beach ball. My eyes welled up with tears. There was a long pause before I could answer her. Her inquisitive little face had no idea what to expect.

"Honey, I will never slap you, no matter what you do, and I would *love it* if you would call me 'daddy'". I supposed I should have addressed this weeks ago, but I was too busy trying to learn how to be a father. I lifted her up and sat her down on my lap. She buried her head in my chest. I stroked her hair and patted her back.

"Good", said the little voice from deep within my chest. "Daddy,…could we have spaghetti for dinner?" Her little voice sung with glee.

"Yes, spaghetti would be a good idea", I answered happily.

I tickled her ribs and made her squirm all over because of how cute her response was.

Chapter 14
"Buttercup's Response"

I was glad we got to go home early. I was glad we got to have spaghetti for dinner for two reasons: the first is because I really liked spaghetti but also because Danny-I mean Daddy and I would always made it together. He would always start by sitting me on the kitchen counter. Then I would break the noodles in half. I would plop them into a big silver pot filled with water. I would measure out some salt in the palm of my hand. I sprinkle it into the pot over the broken spaghetti. My dad would turn on the burner on top of the stove. We would sit there and watch it until the water began to bubble. After it bubbled for a long time, he would pull out a noodle with a fork. I would get to throw it at the wall as hard as I could. As soon as we got a noodle to stick to the wall, it was time to eat. My dad would take some red stuff out of a jar and heat it up in the microwave. Then, he would lift me off of the counter. I would get to set the table, and he mixed the red stuff with the noodles.

Before we ate, Daddy… (I really like saying that. Maybe I will say that again, just cause it's so much fun saying it) *Daddy* would take my fork and knife and cut up the spaghetti on my plate – but it didn't really look like anything was happening. He would cut and cut and cut, but the spaghetti didn't look any different. I wondered how he knew when he was done. I figured it would be one of those things I would understand when I was an adult. But for now, I just wanted to eat my spaghetti.

It would take me a little while to get used to not calling my dad by his first name anymore. I was happy that he let me call him daddy, through. The kids at daycare thought it was weird that I called my father by his first name.

"Why do you call him 'Danny'"? one kid asked.

"Isn't he your father"? another kid asked.

"Maybe he is your step-dad", a third kid said.

Meaghen, a mean girl with blond hair said:

"Maybe he doesn't *love* you enough to let you call him 'Dad'. After all, aren't you like an orphan, or something like that? Maybe he can't wait until you go back to your mother, so he told you to call him by his first name". That made me very sad to think about it.

I knew Meaghen was wrong. Maybe Gloria Jean didn't love me, but I knew that Danny really was my father. I knew that he really did love me. It wasn't because he bought me books and toys and fed me pancakes until I thought I was going to explode – I could tell he loved me just by the way he looked at me. I knew in my heart that he was my father and I knew he loved me. That made me feel safe and warm. That also made me want to sock Meaghen in the stomach, but that isn't what good girls do. This wasn't at all like when I was living in the old building with Gloria Jean. Back then, I never seemed to know what to expect from day to day, minute to minute. Now, I never knew what to expect, either, but it was because my dad was always buying me a new toy or reading a new book to me.

After dinner, Daddy said:

"I have some phone calls to make. Why don't you take 'a first whack' at your essay and I will check in with you in a little while".

I am not sure what that all meant, but I guess it meant that I was supposed to start without him. I couldn't write very well, not real good like the other kids could.

"What should I write about?" I asked him.

"Write whatever comes into your mind. We can refine it later", he said.

He used words that I didn't know what they meant a lot.

I got some paper and a pencil out of his desk and started writing:

> I have a nice dad. He does things with me like take me to the park and push me on the swings. We make spaghetti together. It is better than when I lived in the old building with my mother, Gloria Jean. She slapped me once on the face. It didn't hurt that much, but it made me cry. I hope I can live

> with my dad from now on and not
> have to go back to begging for
> money with Gloria Jean.

After my dad made a bunch of phone calls, he came over and put his arm around me and looked at the piece of paper over my shoulder.

"Let's see what you have, there Hemingway", he said and he picked up my piece of paper. He read it for a long time. His eyes got sorta watery and red. He swallowed real hard.

"Well", he said, as he put the paper back down on the desk, "I like it – but let's leave out the part about how you used to live in the theatre and that your mother slapped you. Let's make this be a happy story." A smile came across his face.

"Should I write a different story?" I asked.

"No. Just make some changes to the one you already wrote", he said. "Leave in the 'spaghetti stuff' and the swings, but not so much living in the old building and begging for money".

"Okay", I replied. It was hard to put all of my thoughts onto a piece of paper. They would get mixed up in my head and I would want to write down everything all at once. When I told that to my dad, he said:

"Don't feel bad, Sweetie, Hemingway had the same problems, and look at how well he turned out". Some day I would like to meet this "Hemingway" guy. I wonder if he worked at the office with my dad.

Chapter 15
"Gloria Jean Reappears"

If anyone ever tells you rehab is fun, punch them in the face for me. It is a gut-wrenching nightmare. The only thing that was good about it was I didn't have to make a single decision – of any kind. People told me what to wear, when to get up and what to do. There were even case workers who told me how I should feel.

Around my first week in rehab, I realized that I probably left Buttercup alone on a swing in Galagher Park. Weeks later, I had a vague recollection of Danny being there, too. After another week or so, it occurred to me what happened: I had what little common sense that was left in my whacked-out head to contact Buttercup's father and turned her over to him. Come to think if it, he never did say that he would take her. I hope she wasn't still sitting there on that swing! If I had more of my state of mind about me, I would have tried to find a rich family who would give me some money for her. I know how that must sound; it must sound like I am trying to sell my daughter like she a used car, but it could be better for her. She would have someone who could give her a normal life. It would be good for the family, too, because she was a pretty cute kid. I both loved her and hated her for it. I loved her because, well, because she *was* my daughter after all, but I hated her because she looked like him. As weird as this will sound, I also hated her because she had my girlish good looks, which, on me were quickly disappearing. Giving Buttercup to a rich family might even be equally bad for me, too. If I had a pile of money, I may be able to be on my own longer, and not have to go into this Hell-hole rehab facility. With a bunch of money, I may have died from an overdose of heroine. All things being said, things seemed to have worked out for the best.

In group therapy sessions, I told the group about my daughter, and that she was staying with my "estranged husband" until I got better. That wasn't the biggest fabrication I have ever manifested; bigger ones were right around the corner, but I think they would have been all over me if I told them the true story. To make me sound like less of a fiend, I sugar-coated it a little and told the group that he may have coerced me into relinquishing her to him. I think, in other group sessions, I may have alluded to the fact that he threatened to either beat me up or go to the authorities if I didn't turn her over to him (the story changed depending on my mood). I also alluded to the fact that he may have confessed to me fantasies of having unnatural relations with children. None of that was true, we never had any type of conversations, of any kind about children, not even if he liked them or not. If, however, it made me seem like less of a monster and more like a "caring mother", I went with it.

Eventually, they determined that I was ready for the next step. That involved me moving into a half-way house and getting a job. I couldn't remember the last time I had a job. None of that really mattered. They would find me the job and tell me where I was going to live. They were, however, pretty adamant about the fact that Buttercup had to come back and live with me. I figured it was a condition of living in the half-way house, you know that: "resume your responsibilities" stuff, so I went along with it. I could always shove her off onto someone else, anyway. Who knows, maybe in six months I would be back on the streets and I could go through with my plan to try to sell her.

They shoved form after form under my nose and told me to sign them. "Don't worry, Mrs. McCullen", they told me, "we will get your daughter back for you". "It is *Miss* Novak", I would answer and keep on signing. Part of me was curious to see how badly her father screwed up the whole "Buttercup situation" and part of me just wanted to get out of this antiseptic, antibacterial-ridden prison and back to somewhere where I could have some real fun.

Chapter 16
"Danny Makes Plans"

The thought never occurred to me that my "crack-head" ex-girlfriend might actually get out of the hospital some day and imagine that she would get custody of Buttercup. What kind of right-thinking government would let a woman who was living in an abandoned building with her five-year old daughter regain her daughter back? Forget about the fact that she had a drug problem, whether she was cured of it or not. Also, let's not forget, this was the same woman who met me in the park and said "There she is - she's the one on the swing – hope everything works out alright" and left! She gave her away without so much as even asking me if it was alright. She didn't even look back to see if I didn't run out the park in the opposite direction without her.

If the thought never occurred to me that Gloria Jean would never actually be able to pry Buttercup away from me, the thought *really* never occurred to me that I would fall so deeply, madly in love with Buttercup. Sometimes in the middle of the night, I would stand in the doorway of Buttercup's room and watch her sleep. Her every move, her every gesture and syllable made me more hopelessly in love with her. Now, the Wicked Witch was about to "huff and puff and blow *my* house down?" Not in this lifetime, I thought, remembering Sam's quote.

I called Toodles up at home that night.

"I have good news and bad news", I told her.

"Well you know me, I am a sucker for 'good news'", she said, in her typical snotty attitude.

"Take tomorrow off", I said.

"…and the bad news?" She said, waiting for the other shoe to drop.

"I have to hide Buttercup", I retorted.

"At *my* house", remarked Toodles.

"Yes", I answered.

"With *ME"* she remarked even snottier.

"…Ah, yes", I managed to eek out.

"Well, it looks like there *is* no bad news", she bellowed.

"Remind me to give you a raise", I said smugly.

"You can't *give* me a raise, you are going to *jail*", she said, with even more attitude than before.

As I was dropping Buttercup off at Toodles' house, Sam called me on my cell phone. He asked me to stop by his office. I went to his office even before I went to my own.

"Danny, you don't have to worry about getting arrested", Sam said. "Carlson knows people in the D.A.s office and they assured us that they have *actual* criminals to arrest".

"Well, that is a relief" I replied. "I have you and your people to thank for that", I answered.

Sam looked hard at me. "It is what we *do,* Danny! This place may seem like just offices and desks and chairs, but we are a *family* here!" He broke off with his sentimentally charged statement. "We responded with so many counter complaints that it will take them a week just read them", he continued. "But one thing is for sure, they will come after you,". Sam was deadly serious. "Danny, we would love to keep torturing City Hall…" Sam went on, but I interrupted him.

"No, of course not. I have to find a lawyer" I butted in. "Got any suggestions?"

"Let me put it to you this way, if I were you, if that was my little girl and someone told me they were going take her from me, I would get the best", he went on. "And in my book, no one is better in these types of cases than Benjamin Solomon", Sam continued.

"Benjamin Solomon!" I said his name like it was the Messiah. "He sounds like a man for the challenge", I went on.

"He will suck the blood out of anyone's veins within 50 feet of him", Sam spewed. "The only place you want to be is on *his* side". There was nothing tentative in Sam's voice.

Chapter 17
"Benjamin Solomon"

I made the first appointment I could with Benjamin Solomon Esq., which was 3 days away at 10:45 in the morning. Buttercup would be in school, and she wouldn't know anything about it. Like every lawyer I have ever known, he worked in a huge office building, very opulently decorated.

His secretary greeted me warmly when I arrived and invited me to have a seat. She picked up her phone and said:

"Mr. Solomon, Mr. Cullen is here". After a pause she said "I will tell him that". She hung up the phone and told me that Mr. Solomon will be with me shortly.

After a few minutes, the office door directly behind the secretary opened. A large man both tall and wide walked out. He wore a suit that had to cost two thousand dollars. His salt and pepper hair was offset by his designer glasses.

"Mr. Cullen, it is a pleasure meeting you, although not under these circumstances". His presence was commanding. I could see why Sam recommended him. "Won't you come in my office?"

I explained how Barbara D. McCullen, a 5 year old child, who I didn't even know was even alive 3 months ago, was thrust on me by her drug dependent mother. I showed him the birth certificate and the few scraps of paper Gloria Jean gave me. I then gave him the order from the state requiring me to return Buttercup to her mother, along with the restraining orders that Sam and company drafted.

After looking at this mixed bag of paperwork, he looked at me for a long time. "Mr. Cullen", he said, "I don't believe in mincing words, or in giving anyone any false hope". I didn't like the sound of that. "Government agencies are very unlikely to separate mothers from their children, almost regardless of how negligent they are", he said.

I started to interrupt but he waved me off saying:

"I don't want you think that, in any way I agree with them, but that is the way it is. The police could find an infant baby crawling into the street and return the baby to the mother's house to find that mother shooting up heroine and the state would eventually return the child to her. It is not right, but it is a cold hard fact of life". His words were unwavering.

"Are you recommending that I grab up my daughter and run?" I asked.

"Absolutely not", he stated. "That would make you a fugitive from the law. Arrest warrants would be issued and you would be a hunted man for the rest of your life. As soon as you applied for a job and gave the employer your Social Security Number, alarms would go off". He couldn't be clearer.

"What I recommend you do is retain my firm. We will fight this like 'junk-yard dogs' to keep your daughter living at your house with you. It will be a lengthy process and, I must say an expensive one, but I am not in the habit of losing". He peered into my eyes while he said this.

"Mr. Solomon, I am a man of considerable wealth…but I would sign it all over to you if I can keep my daughter. My money means nothing to me – Buttercup, that is my daughter's nickname, is the only thing that does mean anything to me. I will do everything you tell me to do, if you promise *you* will do everything you can to help me keep her!" My words were sincere. I almost started to cross my heart.

"Then let's start the work today", he stated. "We will petition the court to quash the state's request and have you named as Buttercup's sole caregiver today." It was obvious he was not comfortable calling Barbara D. McCullen "Buttercup".

"I will need you to do two things:" he continued. "Have a talk with 'Buttercup' as soon as possible. Tell her that there is a chance, no matter how slight, that she may have to go back to live with her mother".

I didn't like the sound of that.

"What is the second thing?" I asked.

"Call me Benji. Here is my card". His business card was in his hand. "Call me any time, night or day, weekends, holidays, any time. You will get a bill for our initial retainer. It will be for ten thousand dollars".

I would have written him the check while I was standing there if he wanted. That was the easy part. The hard part was having to tell all of this Buttercup.

Chapter 18
"Preparing Buttercup for the Inevitable"

It was Saturday. I purposely didn't tell Buttercup what we were going to do, which was very unlike me. I woke her up at 8:30, which was a little earlier than usual for a weekend.

"Is it time to go to school?" her sleepy little voice asked, as she rubbed her eyes.

"No, you little monster", I cackled, "It is Saturday. There *is* no school. Today is 'National Buttercup Day'. We will *celebrate*!" She threw her arms around me and hugged me.

For breakfast, we had waffles and blueberry syrup, which made me a little sick to look at it, but she loved it. We went to the zoo and spent hours looking at every type of animal there was. She loved the Polar Bears. When we went past the gift shop, I bought the biggest stuffed Polar Bear in the store. It was almost the same size as her.

"Murgatroid will be jealous", she said.

"I am sure Murgatroid will learn that there is enough love in your heart for both of them", I quipped.

We went into a tent where live butterflies flew around. One landed on Buttercup's nose. She wrinkled her nose and laughed as she tried to look cross-eyed to try to see it. We saw the dolphin show and rode the train. At some point, she was too tired to walk, so I put her on my back and carried her, sandwiching the bear between her me.

After we had seen everything in the zoo, I took her to her favorite toy store and told her she could pick out 3 toys. That was 2 more than she normally got on a Saturday but I had to prepare her for bad news.

After the toy store, I took her to the girls clothing store, where she tried on beautiful sun dresses and flowered dresses. We even picked out one that had a matching flowered scarf. We bought almost everything she tried on.

"When I wear this dress, Murgatroid can wear the scarf, she said. "That way, he won't be mad at me for Beanie".

"Who is Beanie?" I asked.

She looked at me with amazement. "My *Bear*", she said.

"Oh, Beanie the *Bear",* I finished the thought. Her logic about the scarf was pretty well-formed for a 5 year-old.

With toys, a bear and new clothes under our arms, I asked Buttercup if she wanted to have pizza for dinner. She must have felt like she just won the Lottery.

When we went to restaurants, I always made sure we sat in booths. I would put her in the booth first and then I would slide in after her. That way, no one could get to her without going through me first. It may seem silly, but I had a right to be overly cautious. I never knew what to expect next.

All of this, the zoo, the toys, and the butterflies all led up to one thing. It was time for me to have a "come to Jesus" talk with Buttercup, as my Irish grandmother used to say. I knew it would be necessary to choose my words very carefully, so I had been rolling around a little non-threatening, no-blame speech in my head.

"Buttercup, I want to talk to you about something", I said, as calmly as I could.

"I haven't been taking anybody's things! Honest!" There was sincerity and panic in her voice.

"No, Sweetie, I know that you haven't", I said. "Honey, Gloria Jean is all better now. She would like it if you would go to live with her. Would you like that" I asked. Her eyes fell down onto the table.

"Umm…no…Dad, I don't think so", her little voice trailed off, as she finished her sentence.

"Well", I interjected, "what if it were different this time?"

"What do you mean different", she asked.

"Well", I told her, "Better! Better than before!"

She looked deep into my eyes and let out a huge sigh. "Do *you* want me to go live with her?" Buttercup's voice was the voice I heard whenever she was afraid and sad.

So much for the prepared speech, I thought. "No! I *never* want you to leave me, *ever*!" I made my words be as incontrovertible as possible. "I want you to stay with me!" I stopped short of asking her what she wanted to do, because it may not be up to her or me.

"Maybe…*just* maybe, you *may* have to go live with her…but I am going to try to make it so you *won't* have to go away", I said. Her face got very sad.

"Dad", she started, "I've been good…*real* good! I do what Ms. Johnson says and I never be bad or nothing…Honest!"

"Sweetie", I tried to reassure her, "I know all of that. But things may happen that will be out of my control".

"Will it be today?" she whimpered.

"No, it won't be today. It may take weeks or months or it may never happen, ever". I tried to give her the news as matter-of-factly as I could. "You may have to talk to people…adults…to tell them how you feel…about…where you want to live…about how you would rather live with me". I said that half afraid she would say she didn't. "If you do, will you be scared?" I asked.

"Yes, but I will do it anyway" she said. "They will have to be pretty tough, to take me away…from you". She was repeating what I said about the Irish cop the day I met her. I got a little teary to hear her say that.

"Yes", I agreed. "They will have to be *very* tough, Sweetheart!"

"Daddy, will you be there when I have to talk to the people?" Her little mind raced to understand these inevitabilities.

"I will be *right* there", I chimed. "And another very nice man named Mr. Solomon will be there, too. He is a lawyer who I hired so that you can stay living with me. He will make sure, just like me, that the people aren't mean to you". I wanted to get off that subject as soon as I could. I continued. "But let's not worry about that now, would you like some ice cream?" Ice cream was about the only thing I could think of to turn this acrimonious situation into a pleasant one.

"Yes…, but I can't eat any more", she said innocently. I loved stuffing this kid with food. I guess, in my own way, it was me showing her that I loved her.

"Okay", I said with a chuckle. "We will stop and get movies and pick up some ice cream and have it tonight".

"Can we get sprinkles?" Everything was so easy with her.

"Sure! Sprinkles it is".

That night, she sat scrunched up next to me on the couch, under the blanket, eating ice cream and watching one children's movie after another. If only I could make every one of her troubles disappear with sprinkles, I thought.

Chapter 19
"Going to Court"

Just as Sam had told me, the state would pursue, what they thought, was a reasonable solution to what they saw as a problem: a child without a mother. This flew in the face of the fact that 'said mother' was a recovering drug addict (I would give her the benefit of the doubt), who had a long history of raising a child on the streets. What Sam or Benji failed to tell me is that they would try to wear me down. I would get called into court, sometimes with Buttercup, sometimes without. We would sit in court, sometimes for hours, only to have a recess called and finally have court adjourn for the day without anything happening all day. Buttercup occupied her time by drawing a picture of everything in sight.

I was questioned, re-questioned, examined, re-examined, required to attend pre-trial motions, forced to listen to expert testimony and forced to listen to expert testimony that refuted the previous expert testimony. Benji's examination for me would be relatively simple.

"Mr. Cullen, in your own words, tell us how it is that Barbara McCullen happened to come to live with you. What plans and steps have you made toward securing a normal life for her?" The rest was up to me. Some people in the courtroom actually gasped when I told the judge that Buttercup used to hide food in the pockets of her clothes, and initially preferred sleeping the closets out of fear of being "taken away".

The lead council for the state was Charles Whitcomb, a strange looking man. His suits didn't seem to fit him very well and he looked as though he didn't know what kind of style of clothes he wanted to wear. He wore black shoes with brown suits and ties that didn't match his shirts with shirts that didn't match his jackets. Whitcomb's cross-examination for me was quite a bit more accusatory. I was asked why an adult male would want to raise a young female child. I was asked why Barbara's birth certificate said her name was McCullen and why my last name was Cullen. I was asked how a man, with the demands placed upon him with an occupation such as mine, would find the time to raise a child. Many questions pointed specifically at dishing up dirt on me that didn't exist in the first place, such as:

"How often do you bath the child? When the child bathes, who is present in the room with her? Does the child ever sleep in bed with you? How often does the child sleep in the bed with you? Have you now, or have you ever had thoughts of having inappropriate relations with Buttercup? With any children?" I was glad I heeded Moira's warnings. I could now be strapped to a lie detector and still prove to the world that I was cleaner that Caesar's wife.

Benji did train me well. He taught me to never answer a question put forth by Whitcomb until he had an opportunity to object. He taught me to answer every question with as few words as possible. He trained me not to get baited by those "Tell us, Mr. Cullen, do you still beat your wife, yes or no"? type questions.

Gloria Jean took the stand and wept like a baby, saying the reason that she didn't have the abortion was out of her deep religious convictions. She never has any deep religious convictions all the while I knew her. She stated that the only reason that she had a drug problem was out of the angst of losing her father. She stated that it was out of the fear of her own life that she acted so recklessly as to abandon Buttercup to a man who didn't even know that he had a daughter prior to that day. She further stated that it was out of her deep love for Buttercup that she called me when it was obvious that she would have to enter drug therapy without her. But that was in the past now, according to her, and she was ready to pick up the pieces of her broken life and live it with the verve and vigor of a person who had been given a second chance. I didn't believe a word of it.

In Benji's cross examination, he pounced on Gloria Jean like she was Adolph Hitler himself.

"You lived in an abandoned building? You made Barbara sleep in a closet? You pan-handled money as your only method of a livelihood? How long were you addicted to Heroine? How much of the money that you were able to take in through panhandling was spent toward your drug habit and how much was spent in the care and welfare of your child? Did you make plans to have Barbara educated? Was Barbara ever given any health care measures? If the state returns Barbara to you, what guarantee do the people have that you won't return to your old ways?" Whitcomb objected to that last question,

the judge sustained it. He later told me that he didn't care if Gloria Jean answered that question or not, he just wanted to put the notion into the judge's head that all of this may happen again if he returned Buttercup to Gloria Jean.

My sister, Moira was called to the stand to testify. She said under cross examination that when Buttercup first came to live with me, she was traumatized and lacked many of the social interaction skills prevalent in children her age. She went on to state that she had seen a significant improvement in Buttercup's demeanor in the few short months she lived with me. She maintained that she felt that Buttercup was well on her way to being a normal, well-adjusted child. Lynn Johnson was called to the stand, who testified that when Buttercup first came to her daycare center, she was undernourished and untrusting of adults. She had little interpersonal skills, especially when it came to other children. She went on to say that through the daily routine of being in a nurturing environment, both at the daycare center and at home, she saw a vast improvement, both in her physical and her emotional health. Towanda Harrison was called to the stand, who testified under oath that Buttercup behaved much like what she could only categorize as an emotional zombie when she first met her. She elaborated by stating that she had little emotion, be it high or low, and a natural fear of people. During the 3 short months that she had known her, Buttercup developed into a sweet, charming personality that was a genuine pleasure to be with. The sentiment was unanimous; Buttercup was a mess, both physically and emotionally when she was plopped into all of our lives and within a few short months, she was being transformed into a happy, charming little girl.

Finally, there was only one person left to testify. Miss Barbara D. McCullen was called to the stand. Benji objected. The judge overruled the objection. He did warn the Assistant District Attorney that he would shut down the questioning if he inflamed the witness.

They made Buttercup place her hand on the Bible.

“Do you solemnly swear to tell the truth, the whole truth and nothing but the truth?” the bailiff questioned.

“Huh?” Buttercup couldn’t have been more confused if the man tried to swear her in in Spanish.

“Maybe I can help, your Honor”, I said, as I stood up from my seat. “Honey, do you promise not to tell a fib while you are up there?”

“Oh, sure” she said, “I never tell no fibs” as she smiled to the gallery. Her big brown eyes lit up.

The gallery laughed. The judge banged his gavel and demanded order in the courtroom.

“Mr. Cullen, no more outbursts like that will be tolerated”, the judge said.

“Just trying to move things along, Judge”, I said, with a smile.

“Thank you, Mr. Cullen. We have been holding court in this state for the last 135 years without your help, I think we can manage a little while longer”. The judge was less than happy.

Whitcomb began his examination:

"Barbara, if I ask you any questions that you don't understand and you want me to ask them again, I will, just tell me, okay?" Whitcomb's voice was low and reassuring.

Benji leaned over and said in my ear:

"That is the oldest trick in the book", Benji said. "He is going for two different emotions at the same time. He is trying to get Buttercup to trust him, and at the same time make her look addle-minded. He will ask her questions that no one could answer, then when she can't answer them, he will argue that she lacks the requisite skills to communicate. The other side of that 'just ask me to repeat the question' trick is to create a feeling that she is under his spell and the only way off the witness stand is to answer his questions and his questions alone. He doesn't even want her to look to you for any type of reassurance. I will object as often as I can". Benji was a master in the game of "Courtroom Chess" that was unraveling before us. Benji said:

"Stare at her and nod as often as you can. She will need a reassuring face, a smile, whatever support you can give her. Don't take your eyes off of her for a second", Benji went on. "You never can tell when she will be able to look at you for a happy glance and you want to be looking at her when she does".

"Barbara", Whitcomb began, "Or is it 'Buttercup'? Is that the name you liked to be called?" He said it like a department store Santa Claus, who just asked a 2 year old what they would like for Christmas.

"Buttercup", my tiny daughter retorted.

"Where did you get that nickname from?" Whicomb spewed.

"I don't know", Buttercup answered, in a confused voice.

"Isn't it true that your mother gave you that nickname when you were a baby?" His words were sharp and mean.

"Objection, your Honor". Benji was on his feet before Whitcomb could finish the question. "Asked and answered, your Honor. Barbara already stated that she doesn't know where the nickname came from".

"Move on, Mr. Whitcomb", the judge retorted.

"Buttercup, do you recognize anyone in this courtroom?" he asked.

"Sure", said Buttercup, in her usual cheery way, "I recognize *everyone* in this courtroom", she said as a bright smile spread across her face. The courtroom was sprinkled with laughter.

"How is it that you know *everyone* in the courtroom?" Whitcomb continued.

"Because I am here almost every day", she exclaimed. This caused more laughter throughout the courtroom. The judge banged his gavel.

"Who do you recognize?" Whitcomb continued.

"I recognize, Mr. Solomon and my dad and *you* Mr. Whitcomb!" The gallery laughed again. The judge lightly banged his gavel.

"Do you recognize anyone else?" Whitcomb obviously had an agenda.

"I recognize Murgatroid", Butter said innocently.

"Who is Murgatroid?" Whitcomb sneered.

"My Dog!" At that, Buttercup pulled out her shaggy old stuffed animal from her pocket. A bright smile flashed across her face. The courtroom exploded in laughter.

"Do you recognize the woman sitting at the table", he said, pointing to Gloria Jean.

"Yes". Buttercup stopped in her tracks.

"What is her name?" Whitcomb asked.

"Gloria Jean", Buttercup continued.

"What is she to you?' Whitcomb continued.

"I don't know what that means", Buttercup said, looking down.

"Permission to treat as hostile, your Honor", Whitcomb said.

"We object" Benji hollered. "This is obviously a ploy to confuse a minor child!"

The judge stated, "I will give you a little latitude, but be careful, Mr. Whitcomb".

"Is it not true that the woman sitting at the table, that you identified as Gloria Jean is your mother?"

Buttercup shrugged.

Whitcomb took on his adamant voice again "Well, is she or isn't she?"

"Objection, your Honor, not only is Mr. Whitcomb badgering the witness but it is outside the scope of this witness. She has no way of knowing if Ms. Novak is her mother or not".

Buttercup looked at her shoes, her usual behavior when she was confused or nervous.

"Your Honor, maybe this will help the people get to the bottom of this" Whitcomb continued, "The people would like to enter this document into evidence as Exhibit A". It was the first draft of the "I love my dad" essay Buttercup wrote.

"Do you recognize this?" Whitcomb asked with machine gun precision.

"Yes", Buttercup's voice trailed off.

Whitcomb continued, "Can you tell us why it is that you recognize it?"

"Because I wrote it", Buttercup said, looked back at her shoes.

"Would you please read the highlighted portion?" Whitcomb spouted.

"You mean the part that someone colored over with a yellow crayon?" Buttercup's innocence sent another round of laughter through the courtroom. She looked down and started to read the highlighted portion:

> I have a nice dad. He does things with me like take me to the park and push me on the swings. We make spaghetti together. It is better than when I lived in the old building with my mother, Gloria

> Jean. She slapped me once on the face. It didn't hurt that much, but it made me upset and I cried. I hope I can live with my dad from now on and not have to go back to the theatre with Gloria Jean.

Whitcomb interrupted, "So, do you contend that Gloria Jean IS your mother?"

"Can I be excused?" Buttercup looked worried.

"Not just yet", Whitcomb was not letting her catch her breath.

"Do you contend that Gloria Jean *is* your mother?"

Benji jumped to his feet. "Your Honor, these questions are without merit, irrelevant and have no bearing on this case. Whether Ms. Novak is or is not Ms. McCullen's mother can not be proved or disproved by this witness.

Whitcomb continued, "But her *perception* is what is at question".

"Can I go be by my dad now?" Buttercup was squirming in her chair.

"Not just yet", Whitcomb continued.

"Buttercup, is it not true…"

Whitcomb halted his question in mid sentence, when he saw Buttercup stand up on her chair and face the judge. She waved him over with her hand. She cupped her hand next to the judge's ear and whispered something.

Whitcomb hollered, "Your Honor, the people demand to know what the witness communicated to you".

The judge buried his head in paperwork. "It has no bearing on this case", he said, as he began to wave the bailiff over.

Whitcomb would not be placated. "The people will decide what is relevant. This type of ex parte communication is cause for a mistrial".

The judge looked at Whitcomb. With a disgusted look on his face he said sarcastically, "the *witness* communicated to me that she was afraid she might *poop* in her *pants* if she wasn't excused. Are *the people* satisfied with the answer?" The courtroom exploded in laughter.

Buttercup was escorted to the ladies bathroom by a female bailiff. When she returned, she sat back in the witness chair.

Whitcomb knew that he looked foolish and disregarded the rest of his questions.

"If that is all, Mr. Whitcomb, the witness may step down", the judge said.

"We have a few more questions, your Honor", Benji stated.

"Well, make them brief, Mr. Solomon, it is getting late", the judge sneered.

"Buttercup", he said as he approached the witness stand, "what is Gloria Jean's last name?"

"I don't know" was Buttercup's simple answer.

"What is *your* last name? Benji continued.

"McCullen".

"How long have you known that McCullen was your last name?" Benji continued.

"Ever since I went to live with my dad. I didn't know my first name was really Barbara, either", Buttercup said as she looked at me. "Come to think of it, I didn't even know what 'last names' were until I went to live with my dad". It was obvious to me that she was picking up speech habits from me. Saying things like "come to think of it" would have *never* been part of her vocabulary before she met me.

Benji went on. "You call Ms. Novak 'Gloria Jean', but you call Mr. McCullen 'dad'. Why is that?

"Well", she started, "I used to call him 'Danny' but we had a talk. He said I could call him 'dad' and he wouldn't slap me if I did". She looked at her shoes.

Benji looked surprised. "Slap you?"

Buttercup wiped her nose with her wrist, "Yes, I called Gloria Jean 'mommy' once…she slapped me on my face when I did. She told me to never call her that again".

Benji walked closer to Buttercup and hunkered down near her. In a soft, comforting voice, he said:

"Would you rather live with your dad or Gloria Jean?"

Before she could answer, Whitcomb objected.

"Overruled", the judge stated, "I want to hear this!"

Buttercup's face lit up. "My dad!"

Benji continued. "Why?'

"Because I get toys and clothes and spaghetti", she said excitedly.

"Toys and clothes and spaghetti", Benji repeated. "Is there anything else?"

"Yes, he takes me to the zoo and butterflies land on my nose. We watch movies under the blanket and I get to snuggle up by him. Sometimes, we get ice cream". She looked at the judge. "I like sprinkles on my ice cream". Benji perfectly led Buttercup into a place where she could share with the court how much better her life was with me than it was living with Gloria Jean.

Benji's voice became very soft. "Do you love your father, Buttercup?"

Buttercup never broke her gaze with Benji. "Yes", she stated.

"Does your father love you?" Benji asked.

Before she could answer, Whitcomb objected. "It is beyond the scope of the witness as to whether Mr. Cullen loves this witness", he said.

"Please allow me to rephrase, your honor", Benji continued. "Do you *think* your father loves you?'

"Yes", Buttercup responded.

"Is it because he buys you toys and clothes?" Benji asked.

"No", replied Buttercup.

"Is it because he takes you to the zoo?" Benji continued.

“No”, she went on.

“Then how do you know he loves you?” Benji went on.

Because I just do!” Her little eyes shot directly to me.

“So if someone else bought you toys or took you to the zoo, you would not necessarily love them?” Benji went on.

“That would be nice…but, no…it’s more that than”, Buttercups went on.

“What about this?” Benji went on. “Could you love someone who *didn’t* buy toys or who *didn’t* take you to the zoo?

“If they loved me, I could”. Buttercup was firm in her stance.

“So then, Buttercup”, Benji continued, “how do you know that your father loves you?”

Buttercup looked Benji square in the eye. “I know because he smiles at me a lot when he looks at me. I know because he holds me in his arms and hugs me real tight and I know he won’t let anybody hurt me. I know… because I just know”. At that, she glanced over at me and said “I can’t say it any better than that!”

The room fell eerily silent. No one in the room could move. It was as through everyone in the room was cast into a magical spell through her testimony and even scratching their noses would make the magic go away.

Finally Benji broke the spell when he said: “You said it just fine. We have no more questions for this witness, Benji stated. When Buttercup walked past him, he rubbed her head affectionately.

"The state wishes to recall Gloria Jean Novak", Benji continues.

Gloria Jean took the stand. The Bailiff reminded her that she was still under oath.

Benji looked at her like she was Satan. "Ms. Novak", he began "Barbara maintains that you slapped her on the face once. Are those your recollections, as well?"

"Yes,…but…" Benji cut her off.

"Were you under the influence of an illegal substance when you did it?" His ploy, he told me later, was to remind the judge that not only was she a drug user, but that she had custody of Buttercup when she was under the influence of an illegal substance.

"No, I never shot up in front of Buttercup!" Gloria Jean's comments were empathic.

"Non-responsive, your honor", Benji snapped. "I didn't ask you if you ever 'shot up' in front of Barbara, I asked you of you were under the influence of an illegal substance *when* you struck her?"

"No…no I was not high when I slapped Buttercup", Gloria Jean sniffled out.

"How can you be so sure about that, Ms. Novak?" Benji questioned.

"Because I only shoot up at night…after Buttercup goes to bed", Gloria Jean continued.

"Well, I suppose that makes it, okay, then doesn't it, Ms. Novak"

“Objection”, bellowed Whitcomb.

“Sustained”, the judge said dismissively.

“Do you remember why you slapped her?” Benji was going for the throat.

“She was very sleepy”, Gloria Jean said, beginning to remember the incident. “She said ‘mommy’ can we go home…”

“Where did this take place?” Benji snapped.

Gloria Jean paused. She knew she was getting into more and more trouble as Benji’s questions continued. She looked out the window. “We were on the street”.

“What were you doing? Benji inquired.

There was another long pause. Gloria Jean looked down at the table. “I was getting money”, she said.

“Getting money?” Benji continued. “From an ATM?”

Gloria Jean swallowed hard. “No…from strangers.”

Benji’s head snapped and fixed his gaze on her.

“From strangers?” he asked in an accusatorial way.

“Objection, your Honor”, Whitcomb exploded. “It has already been established that Ms. Novak was indigent and that she pan-handled for money. Counsel is merely trying to inflame the judge with these seamy details.

“Sustained”, the judge remarked “Do you have anything else, Mr. Solomon?”

"Yes, Judge, just one more question", Benji answered. "Why would you slap your daughter's face for asking you if she could go home?"

"I didn't – I didn't slap her face for asking if we could go home. I wanted to go home, too. I slapped her face because I was shocked that she called me 'mommy'. I didn't want my daughter to think of me *as* her mother! I knew the life I was providing her with was a bad one. I didn't want her to think that her mother was such a pitiful person. I didn't want her to think that her mother would subject her to such a miserable life". At that, Gloria Jean started to cry. She took a handkerchief out of her purse and blew her nose.

"So you *knew* that the life you were subjecting your daughter to was, what was your term, 'a miserable life'?" Benji was tightening the noose.

"Yes…but it wasn't my fault", Gloria Jean pleaded.

"It wasn't your fault? Why is that, Miss Novak?" Benji was sucker punching his witness.

"Because my father…" Benji cut her off.

"Because your father killed himself?"

"Yes", she replied.

"So everyone who losses a parent to suicide should live on the streets and shoot heroine? Is that your testimony, Ms Novak?

"Objection" Whitcomb interjected.

"Sustained", said the judge. "Do you have anything else for this witness?"

"Yes, your honor, I do" Benji went on. It is your testimony that you struck your daughter on the face for calling you 'mommy'. And you did that because you didn't want her to think that she was being raised by, as you put it, someone as pitiful as you. Would it be fair to say that you did it for *her own good*?' was Benji's reply.

"Yes", bellowed Gloria Jean.

"*You* slapped your daughter in the face, for calling you *mommy*? And that, you want us to believe it was *for her own good*?" Benji drove Gloria Jean into the mother-load of traps. He might as well have asked her "do you still beat your child, yes or no?"

"If I could change it, I would! I am *sorry* Buttercup!", Gloria Jean cried.

"I will bet you are", Benji stated. "No further questions". Benji walked back to the defense table like he was walking away from a pile of garbage.

"If there are no more questions", the judge continued, "we stand adjourned until 9:30 tomorrow morning.

Whitcomb interrupted. "If it please the court, your Honor, Mr. Solomon's questioning has brought up some new issues that I would like to have clarified. The people would like to recall Barbara McCullen",

"Mr. Whitcomb…" the judge began to say, "What can possibly be gained by putting Barbara back on the witness stand?"

"This won't take long, your Honor". Buttercup remounted the witness stand.

"Barbara", Whitcomb began, "You remember the time 'your mother' slapped you pretty well, don't you?"

"Yes". Buttercup's eyes were transfixed on Whitcomb's as her head nodded up and down.

"Why is that?" Whitcomb continued.

"Because – it made me cry", Buttercup continued.

"Was that the *only* time 'your mother' ever made you cry?" Every time Whitcomb got to 'your mother', he pointed it out with his voice.

"Yes!" Buttercup's lower lip and chin began to quiver.

"Were you ever punished by your mother?" Whitcomb went on.

"No, but I am not sure why not", Buttercup went on.

"What is it you are not sure about?" Whitcomb went on.

"Why I am not punished more", she continued.

"What do you mean by that", Whitcomb asked as he marched across the room.

"Well…I am a bad child", Buttercup elaborated.

"You are a bad child?" Whitcomb asked.

"Yes! I am a bad child! I have no father and no mother and I live in an abandoned building. That is what Gloria Jean told me. She said that if I were a good child, I would have a father and a mother and I would go to school". Buttercup's eyes got glassy.

At that, I reached over to Benji and said "What the Hell has he got her saying? A Bad child? Because she has no mother or father? Benji, make this stop".

Benji said "let him go, he is so over his head right now, there is no way he can win this trial.

Whitcomb went on to ask:

"Is it not true that when Ms. Novak slapped you that it was just an unfortunate occurrence that happens sometimes between a child and her mother and not an indication of child abuse?" Buttercup had no idea what he just asked. She thought that she did something wrong. A look of horror came over her face. She stared at Whitcomb and a tear came to her eye.

At that, I had enough. I jumped up out of my chair.

"Your Honor, *I* don't even know what that ridiculous stream of nonsense means and I graduated from college, how is a 5 year old child supposed to make any sense of it?" I was furious.

"Sit down, Mr. Cullen, or you will be held in contempt. You have a lawyer to represent you here. I am compelling the witness not to answer that question. This court stands adjourned until tomorrow morning".

"The people wish to continue their questioning of this witness tomorrow morning, your honor", Whitcomb interjected.

I sat down. While Benji gathered up his paperwork, I leaned over.

"You *have* to make this *stop*", I whispered. "Buttercup is terrified".

"She is doing fine", Benji said with his usual lawyer grin. "We have the judge on *our* side. Whitcomb stepped into it by introducing that note. By the time we are through, we should be able to have Gloria arrested for child neglect – hey" Benji continued, "why didn't I think of that in the first place"?

"You don't know Buttercup like I do" I said insistently. "She is scared out of her mind. She hates all of this and she is afraid that someone is going to abduct her and take her away from me and make her live in that old building again".

"Don't worry". Solomon said. "He can't keep throwing 'balloon juice' around much longer. We already have Gloria Jean looking like Genghis Khan through Buttercup's testimony and through *her own testimony.* This will be all over in a few more days.

"I hope you are right", I expressed.

"I get paid for being right", Benji said heading for the door.

What we didn't know is that Whitcomb had a card up his sleeve that he was about to play, a card that would change everything.

Chapter 20
"So Low the Ground Looks Up"

There was a text message from Toodles and another one from Chuck Patterson, my boss. Chuck needed to see me about an urgent matter by the end of the day. That was the last thing I needed, was to have to sit across the desk from him and listen to one of his "yeah-rah-team" speeches about how I needed to sell more.

By the time Buttercup and I got back to the office, Toodles had ready left for the day. Buttercup wanted to draw pictures in my office, but I told her that we weren't going to stay that long.

Patterson was still in his office. I knocked on the door as I opened it.

"You needed to see me, Chuck?" He was just hanging up the phone.

"Yes, I do Danny", he said and he shuffled paperwork on his desk. "Do you mind if Buttercup waits outside? Madeline can keep an eye on her". Madeline, Chuck's secretary, never left before he left and he never seemed to leave. I closed the door and sat across from his desk.

"Danny, I know that you have been having troubles lately", he started. "I know that this has been a bad time for you, but your sales are off sharply. We have tried to work with you toward getting them back up, but so far, nothing has worked". His expression was emotionless. "I am afraid we will have to let you go". He didn't blink.

"Let me go? Let me go where", I responded, not quite sure of what he was talking about.

"Danny, we are going to have to terminate your employment here at GLG."

"Chuck, this couldn't come at a worse time", I remarked.

"These things don't seem to ever *have* a good time", he continued. "I never like doing this, but we do have to make a business decision".

I saw there speechless.

I finally formulated a thought. "Don't you know what is going to happen?" I said. "I will just take my clients with me and go to the place down the street. I will be up and running in a week and GLG will suffer the loss, not me!" My logic was that of a desperate man.

"Danny, you hardly have any clients left", explained Patterson. "Your numbers are off by as much as 75%!" His words stuck hard in his throat. "Look, you can stay on through the end of the month, and there will be a 90 day severance package but that is the best I can do.

It was obvious that the decision was made and that there was nothing to talk about. I stood up, shook Chuck's hand and left.

Buttercup and I went home and had hot dogs and potato chips for dinner and watched cartoons on the couch, under a blanket until it was time for her to go to bed.

Problems seemed to be followed by more problems. Court was set to resume at 9:30 but Benji's office called and asked if I could meet him at his office at 8:30. When I got there, Benji was poring over more paperwork.

"The state has come up with a new wrinkle", he said. "It seems they feel that Buttercup can't testify about her state of mind while she is domiciled with you. They feel that she can't be objective about living with you while she is living with you", Benji continued.

"What does that mean?" I inquired.

"It seems they want to suspend the trial for a month. During that time, Buttercup would be placed in foster care". Benji's voice was apologetic. "I can fight this for a while, but it seems like one of those things that we will eventually lose", he stated.

"Can they do that"?, I demanded. "This kid has been screwed over for 5 years, her mother passes her to me like a stray puppy, she moves in with me, I buy her a bear and feed her a couple of hot dogs and now I have to tell her that she is going to go live somewhere else? In foster care?"

Benji tried to calm me down. "They think they are doing the 'right thing'. They aren't used to this kind of case. They are used to cases where crack-head mothers are selling their kids to white slavery rackets".

"Well, believe me, with Gloria Jean at the helm, they may just get their wish", I stated. "Benji, you might as well know this up front", I confided. "I am going to lose my job. Financially, I will be okay for a while, and you will get paid, but…"

"But it doesn't make our case any stronger", Benji answered. "We will have to try to weather out this storm", he said finishing his thought.

Chapter 21
"Moira"

Being Danny's older sister was a little like being the clown at a Rodeo. I was never sure what to expect. None of us had a normal upbringing, but I think he got it worse because he was the only son. Suffice it to say, when he got rid of that drug-addicted girlfriend, it was a good day. When he got out of that goofy record store job and got a job as an investment broker, that was a real good day. I loved Buttercup dearly, but I feared this whole relationship was going to end badly. I wished I had the opportunity to meet her under different circumstances. When he called me and told me how Gloria Jean "delivered" Buttercup to him, I knew we were in for some rough times, and I always suspected that it would come to this sort of ugly ending. After all, Buttercup is a human being; you don't just trade people around like they were baseball cards.

I followed the trial as closely as I could and provided as much assistance as I could, in a professional capacity. As a social worker, I kept a safe distance from the proceedings – for two reasons: the first was, it was not my fight. The second was, I was afraid that there was going to be an unhappy ending. The stage was set for that second part.

It was much like any weekday night. I went to bed around 10:30 with my alarm set for 6:30 so I could be to the office at 8:00. I fell asleep in record time, due to a heavier work load than usual. I was startled out of my sleep by a piercing sound. It was the phone ringing. My first instinct was to look at the clock, which sat on the night stand on the other side of the room in the dark. I could see that it was 2:37 AM. I didn't think to look at the Caller I.D.

"Hello?" My voice cracked as I answered.

"So, what do you know about the foster system?" The voice on the other end sounded like a drunken man.

"Danny?" I was surprised to hear from him at this hour. I was twice as surprised that he was drunk. I don't think he touched a drop of alcohol since Buttercup entered his life.

"Do you know what time it is?" I screamed.

"Sorry", he said "…but desperate times deserve….something….how does the rest of that go? ", He was so drunk that he had trouble formulating his thoughts.

"The Foster system?" I repeated.

"Desperate times deserve the Foster system?" Danny slurred.

"Danny", I spouted, "why are you calling and what do you want to know about the Foster system?'

"The court thinks I am 'Vulcan Mind-melding' Buttercup. They want her to go into foster care for a month…and *then* resume the trial".

"Danny", I interrupted, "Foster care is a good thing when there is evidence of a parent abusing a child, but in this case, it would be the seventh ring of Hell. You could be sending Buttercup to live with Mr. Rogers, and you *could* be sending her to live with the Manson Family" I continued. "There are plenty of people who sign up for as many kids as the state will allow them, just for the money. The kids are hungry, dirty, neglected. They clean them up just in time for their inspections and everyone thinks they are fine". I had no intention of sugar-coating the situation.

There was a long pause. "As if that is not bad enough", I continued, "Buttercup has relationship sustaining issues as it is. If you send her to a foster home, she will think that you are abandoning her, too", I stated. "The damage could be permanent and irrevocable. Even worse than that, Danny, she could hate you for it". The pause this time was even longer. "Get your lawyer to get a stay of execution and we will find case law against moving her", I continued.

"There will be no stay, no further delays. They get her next Thursday", Danny blurted out. My heart sunk.

"That is crazy", I exclaimed. "That is about the worst decision I have ever heard". There was nothing tentative in my voice.

"Everything in this case has been the worst decision *somebody* has ever heard", my younger brother said. "I have to pack her cases and give her up next Thursday. "Anyway, I better let you get back to sleep" he said as he hung up the phone.

I laid there looking at the ceiling until the alarm went off at 6:30.

Chapter 22
"Danny's Decision"

I read up as much as I could about the foster care situation. While the state provided beautiful color brochures stating that foster care saved more than one child's life, there were many instances cited on-line of kids being abused, mistreated and, in some cases lost in the system. Parents who have had their children admitted into foster care went back to reclaim them, to find that they were no longer with the family that they were placed in the care of. They were transferred to other foster care parents, sometimes again and again. More than one parent said that relocating their children was a strolling nightmare. Some said they never found them. Foster care, as far as I was concerned, was not an option. It was time for me to let Gloria Jean have custody of Buttercup. I figured giving up the fight was the devil I knew.

Benji was not happy with my decision, but at least he understood it. Buttercup would be placed under the parental supervision of Gloria Jean, to be dragged around with her through as many life changes as she chose to undertake. We would ask the state to mandate regular visits and inspections in an effort to try to safeguard that Gloria Jean would not return to her previous ways, and to assure me that Buttercup was being cared for. Everyone told me that such an arrangement looked good on paper, but it would be easy for Gloria Jean to skip them and disappear entirely with very little effort. I would agree to cease my claim toward the parental care of Buttercup, in exchange for visitation rights. Believe it or not, that was the easy part. The difficult part was how to tell Buttercup.

We went to the park and Buttercup and Murgatroid played on the monkey bars and went on the swings for hours. After the park, we went to one of those chain-restaurant, pizza parlor/children's theme parks for dinner. She and I and six other kids played in the ball pit. The mothers of the other children thought it was weird for me, a grown man, to be *in* the ball pit with a collection of kids, but if they knew the kind of message I had to deliver, they would be in the ball pit with me.

When we got home, Buttercup took a bath, and put on her favorite pajamas. I dried her hair with a hair dryer. I was so sad at what I knew I had to do that I could barely look at her. When we were done, we took out seat on the couch under the blanket. She reached for the remote, but before she could turn the television on, I said:

"Honey, I need to talk to you about something". She could see the worry in my eyes.

"Sweetie", I continued, "remember the conversation that we had about Gloria Jean getting better? Well, she is. She is much better than she was. And guess what?
She misses you. She lives in a big house with a lot of nice new friends". That was probably the first time a half-way house was ever described so opulently.

"She would like it if you would go live with her for a while", I said. Her face was confused and sad.

"But I want to stay here", her little voice whimpered.

"Honey, I want you to stay her too, but maybe you will like it at Gloria Jean's house". I tried to paint as rosy of a picture as I could.

"Will I have to live in that old building again…" she started to say.

"*No*!" I exclaimed. "You will *never* go back *there.* You will *never* be treated like that again", I confided.

"Do I have to go now", she whimpered.

"No, Honey! You get to sleep in your bed tonight. Gloria Jean wants you to go live with her on Thursday."

Her eyes welled up with tears and a big blob of tear drop landed on her cheek. She was so sad, she was speechless.

Without thinking, I completely let down my guard. "Honey, I am so sorry!" Now tears ran down my cheeks. I was so sad I didn't know what to do.

"I don't want to watch T.V." her little voice said. "Is it alright if I just sit her and talk to Murgatroid for a little while?"

"Of course it would". I stared at Buttercup for a long time. Finally, I got up and started toward the kitchen to give her some quiet time with Murgatroid. She had already pulled the stuffed animal out of the pocket of her pajamas and was talking to it. It was the same face I saw when I first met her on the swing 3 months ago. She seemed to sooth herself through her quiet conversation with this bit of cloth and stuffing. I wished I had a "Murgatroid", because I suddenly felt all alone, as all alone as I ever have felt in my life.

After watching her talk to her stuffed dog for almost ten minutes, I thought "This is crazy! She is sad and I am sad", I thought to myself. "You are the adult", the thoughts continued to run in my head, "Fix this!"

"Buttercup? Would you like to watch T.V. with me in my bed?" She had never been allowed in my bed before because of that "watchful eye" nonsense. But all of that was behind us now. If they were going to take her away from me anyway, no one would know or care where she slept a few days before she would be taken away. After all, they were about to take her away anyway, even through I did everything right. Why deprive both of us of what every 'normal' parent takes for granted?

Her head turned to look at me slowly. "Your bed?" she said.

"Uh huh", my mood never faltered.

"Can Murgatroid come, too?" he tiny little voice questioned.

A large smile grew across my face. "Of course he can", I stated.

"Okay", she said. She looked down at her stuffed animal. "Let's go, Murgatroid", she said as she started walking toward me. When she reached me, I picked her up and ran down the hall with her in my arms, to her squeals of delight. When we got the bedroom, I gently threw her down on the bed and started tickling her, which made her squirm and squeal some more. I stopped and stared at this precious gift from God and kissed her on the forehead. Even through I was completely dressed, I dragged her to the head of the bed and laid her head across my chest and pulled the covers over us. I grabbed the remote and turned on the television.

Within 15 minutes, Buttercup was sound asleep. One thing I will say about that child is she loved to sleep. When I sure she was asleep, I changed the channel to the evening news. Amid the stories of murder, mayhem and buildings burning down, there was a story that I found particularly interesting. The news woman with the permanent smile reported:

> "And after almost 50 years in business, the Scarlatti Vintage Record Store is scheduled to close its doors. The owner, Tony Scarlatti is ready to retire, but can't find anyone to continue on with his work. After 47 years in the business, The Scarlatti Vintage Record Store will close. Several investment firms are currently placing bids on the property".

"Tony Scarlatti", I said out loud to nobody. "There was a medieval composer named Antonio Scarlatti", I continued.

Buttercup's sleepy voice said, "What, Daddy?"

"Nothing, Sweetie", I said under my breath. Go back to sleep", I said as I kissed her head.

Chapter 24
"The Day of Reckoning"

Benji, over several meetings with Charles Whitcomb, tried everything to allow Buttercup to avoid the foster home situation by living with Gloria Jean for one week and then me for one week. The state, he reported, would not hear of that. Then, Benji proposed "Monday through Friday with Gloria Jean and Weekends with me". Whitcomb didn't like that either. As good as he could make it was I would get "supervised" visitation every other weekend for 4 hours. I, the investment consultant, was being treated like a criminal and the criminal was being treated like a queen. This turn of events eluded me for its irony.

Benji and Whitcomb could cook up anything they wanted but the final decision would be up to the judge. A motion hearing was scheduled to present our new arrangement.

I dressed Buttercup in her favorite Hawaiian dress. Toodles came over and curled her hair and put the matching ribbon from the dress in her hair. There was even enough material left over to make a collar for Murgatroid. Buttercup looked like she had just stepped out of a children's clothing catalog.

Once court was called to order, Benji approached the bench.

"If it please the court, your Honor, a motion has been brought before the court which hopefully will spare any further pain and suffering to any of the parties and will save a lot of the court's time. The agreement is spelled out in this motion".

Benji handed the paperwork to the bailiff, who handed it to the judge. The judge paged through the document. "Before your Honor rules on it, my client would like to make a statement", Benji stated.

“Proceed”, the judge stated, placing the paperwork down on the desk in front of him.

I stood up and swallowed hard.

“Your Honor, if it please the court, I never asked to be a father. The thought of having a child of my own never even occurred to me. Yet, as soon as I met Buttercup, something in me changed. I changed for the better. Now, I am not wholly interested in myself anymore. My interest, my thought and my attention have been drawn solely and entirely onto my daughter. I find myself seeing random things like pencil sharpeners and I think, ‘I wonder if Buttercup knows what that is?’ The goody tray rolls by at work and I think ‘I wonder if Buttercup would like peanut soufflé bars?’ There was no way that someone could have told me 3 months ago that I would feel like this, about anyone or anything…but I do. She is the first face that I see in the morning and the last face that I see at night.

For some reason, this court feels that men can’t raise children; that child-rearing is an exclusive right for women only. That is as crazy as thinking that ‘men should go to work and women should stay home’.

Regardless of how this court feels, or maybe because of how this court feels, I am placed in a precarious situation. The situation is: should I continue to fight selfishly for what I would like, or should I do what is best for the other people in this equation, in this case, my daughter. This fight could go on for months, years, and Buttercup could get transferred from one foster home to the next until she had no idea who I am *or* who her mother is or even who *she* is.

I have decided, today, to end this fight. I have decided today to stop being selfish. It is time for Ms. Novak, and I to continue on with our regular lives, and time to grant Barbara McCullen one of her own. There is only one way that I can see that of happening: I would like this court to consider granting custody of Barbara D. McCullen to her birth mother, Gloria Jean Novak. I would, however, beseech the court to not take her out of my life completely. Please, Judge, please consider the visitation right outlined in the brief before you.

I would like to thank the court for their understanding in this matter", I said, ending my speech.

The judge staring at me in silence for a long time.

"Do you realize, Mr. Cullen, that this decision would be irreversible? There would be no revisiting it later", he said.

"I understand, your Honor", I told him.

"Fine", the judge continued. "This matter will take some time to consider. We will stand in recess until Monday". He stood and left the courtroom.

Feeling as badly as I had in weeks, I turned to walk back to the table with Benji and Buttercup. I could see Gloria Jean and Whitcomb celebrating across the aisle from me. Buttercup was playing with Murgatroid on the defense table, detached from the proceedings. I think she felt that I betrayed her by sending her away. She was revisiting her relationship with the only true friend she felt she still had left.

As the judge left the court room, I handed some paperwork to Benji. "Could you take care of another small matter for me?", I asked. "It isn't exactly the crime of the century or anything, but maybe you can figure out how to expedite it.

Chapter 25
"Gooley Cheese Sandwiches"

Benji asked me if he could take us out to lunch.

“Thanks for the offer, but I think I would like some ‘alone time’ with ‘you know who’”, I replied.

“I understand”, Benji remarked.

The “all-night diner” at the corner was the closest restaurant to the court house.

We got a booth against the windows. There was an awkward silence between us. It was finally broken when Buttercup said: “I like wearing ribbons in my hair. Do you think I look good with this ribbon?” She was obviously looking for things to talk about.

“Yes, I do, Sweetie”, I answered. “Do you remember when we went to breakfast that day?” I said. I knew she would.

“Daddy…did I do something bad? I kept my promises, didn’t I?” I could feel my heart break.

“No, Sweetie”, I said, “You did not do anything bad. And remember that stuff you said in court? About being a bad child. It isn’t true. None of it is true. It isn’t your fault that you had no father and that you lived in that old building. You are a remarkably wonderful child and I love you”. At that, I started to cry. “Buttercup, I am so sorry you had to live like that. If I knew what was going on, I would have stopped it, I swear!”

Buttercup’s face was comforting. “That’s okay, daddy. You didn’t know. At least I had a dad for a little while!”

No, Buttercup”, I interrupted, “I will *always* be your father…and I will *always* love you…..no matter what happens…no judge, no court, no ‘anything else in the world’ could ever change that”.

There was a long silence, which was fine with me because I got a chance to wipe the tears from my eye and blow my nose. Finally, the silence was broken.

"What if I don't like it?" She asked.

"With Gloria Jean?" I asked.

She just nodded.

"Then, I will figure out some way to fix it", I answered.

"Do you *promise"?* she asked.

I didn't say a word. I just took my right finger and crossed my heart.

"I still get to come and see you don't I? You and Toodles and Mr. Solomon?"

"Well", I retorted, "maybe not Mr. Solomon!"

"Can I have gooley cheese?" Somewhere along the way, she began to call grilled cheese sandwiches "gooley cheese".

"Sure you can", I answered.

Chapter 26
"Entering the Plea for the Record"

It was decided. Buttercup would wear ribbons in her hair. It was the easiest decision I was able to make in the days to come. Everyone on my side of the fight would wait on pins and needles to see what the judge would dream up in regards of our most recent petition.

Monday morning finally came, at last. Buttercup was adorned in clothes as cute as any child ever wore, complete with a brightly colored ribbon in her hair. Murgatroid also had a matching scarf around his neck. When we got to court, Benji was already at defense table.

"The bailiff said we should expect the judge any minute now", Benji said.

"How do you think he will rule?" I asked.

"These Muni judges usually do whatever the ADA recommends" Benji responded.

"All rise", the bailiff stated.

The judge sat down and filed through the motions that Benji presented to him last week. After a long pause, he began to speak.

Finally, the bailiff indicated that court was about to be recalled into session and instructed everyone to rise. The judge walked in carrying an arm-load of paperwork under his arm and plopped it down on the desk in front of him. After arranging the paperwork, he took off his glasses, and began to speak.

"Decisions", he began, "involving minor children are never easy. While things can look a certain way in the courtroom, they can be very different in the home. While many people in my chair would merely apply the law with an even hand and follow the precepts of New York case law, it strikes me that the greater issue, specifically the future of a 5-year old girl, would not, or may not be met if I did. While Mr. Whitcomb, Mr. Solomon and I are all experts in the law, we are hardly experts in psychology or in the matters of social work. The options, as I see them, are thus: send Barbara to a foster home while this trial continues or grant guardianship to her birth mother. It is because of that, that I have asked a New York-appointed social worker to examine the case file and to help me in rendering a decision. Again, I hardly feel confident to render a decision without consulting all of the experts available. I have asked Ms. Dorothy Raetzke to review this case over the weekend and to speak, not on behalf of either side, but to merely provide an opinion on how either option would effect Ms. McCullen. At that, the court will hear from Ms. Raetzke.

At that, the door to the courtroom opened and a woman with blonde curly hair walked in. As soon as Buttercup saw her, her eyes lit up.

"Dorothy!" She almost jumped out of her chair. Looking into the gallery, the woman looked back, put her glasses on and said:

"Nola? Is that you?"

"No", Buttercup remarked. "Yes…but no…my name isn't Nola! My name is Buttercup…Well, really it is Barbara."

The court was adrift with noise and commotion. The judge banged his gavel on his desk and called for the court to come to order.

"That's Dorothy?" I asked. "I thought she was make-believe. Do you mean there really is a Dorothy"?

"Yes, Dad. She used to read to us in the park and let us color and told us…well how to play make-believe games".

Dorothy said, "Your Honor, I would like a moment with No…ahh Barbara." The judge motioned for her to approach Barbara. Dorothy walked over to our table, never taking her eyes off of Buttercup. When she was right in front of our table, she looked at me and smiled and said.

"Hello, I am Dorothy Raetzke."

"I am very pleased to meet you, Ms. Raetzke. If you don't mind my asking, how is it that you happen to know my daughter?"

"Well, let's just say that it is a long story, but I have known her for months. I met her while I was conducting a reading program through the New York City Performing Arts Department. Do you mind if I have a few words with her?" My face must have been full of trepidation, which caused Ms. Raetzke to say,

"It will be fine, Mr. Cullen. I am here to remedy this situation, not make it worse."

"Well", I started to say "if you don't mind, I will stay right here with you while you do". Ms. Raetzke unlocked her gaze from Buttercup and looked at me.

"Of course, sir", she began. "This will only take a minute and what I have to ask her you can be here for." She bent down so she was eye to eye with Buttercup. "Barbara, is it?" Buttercup's head bobbed up and down.

"She likes to be called B-", I started to say.

"Yes, Mr. Cullen, I gathered that. Buttercup, why did you tell me your name was Nola?"

Buttercup looked scared. "Please don't be mad at me, Dorothy! I'm sorry!"

"You didn't do anything bad, Buttercup, and I am not mad at you. But, why did you tell me your name was Nola?"

"I didn't", Buttercup said in a soft tone. "You asked me what my name was. Gloria Jean…that is my mother…kinda…lady…told me that I shouldn't tell people what my name was. If I did, they may take me away. So I said 'no name'. I'm sorry, Dorothy. I must have said it too soft. Are you mad at me now?"

Dorothy paused a long pause. "No, Buttercup, I am not mad at you. Thank you for straightening that out for me." Dorothy turned and faced the judge. "Thank you for allowing me some latitude".

At that, Benji stood up. "If it please the court, I would like a recess called so that counsel can be brought up to speed on this recent development.

"An excellent idea", the judge said. "I will see Ms. Raetzke and both lawyers in chambers. We are recessed for one hour.

At that, the judge, Benji, Whitcomb and Dorothy all disappeared into a room behind the judge's desk. It felt like we were just hit by a cyclone and this was the calm after the storm. The silence was finally broken by Buttercup's little voice.

"Where'd Dorothy go?" she asked.

"I don't know…I mean I know, but I wonder what is going on. Buttercup, why didn't you tell me that Dorothy used to read to you?"

"I did, Dad", Buttercup did. "She taught me how to read. You never believed me".

Scratching my head, I said "I guess you did tell me that! Sorry! I guess I thought you made her up."

"No, Dad, she is real".

After about an hour, Benji came back out. He tapped me across the thigh with some rolled-up papers.

"You are gonna like this", he said, as he took his seat.

The judge sat down and indicated to the bailiff to swear Dorothy in. “Mr. Solomon, do you have any questions for this witness?”

Benji stood. “Yes, I do, your Honor. For the record, Ms. Raetzke, please give your full name to the court”.

“Of course. My name is Dorothy Louise Raetzke.”

“And what do you do for a living?” Benji asked. .

“I am a social worker. I am employed by the city of New York. I conduct a reading program for children in the park.”

“That sounds like a very admirable profession, Ms. Raetzke”, Benji continued.

“Actually, it is Doctor Raetzke”, Dorothy continued.

“*Doctor* Raettzke”, Benji continued. “Could you tell this court about your education?”

“Yes”, Dorothy continued. “I have a Master of Science in Education. I specialize in educating children from broken homes. Many of them are indigent, such as in Barbara’s case, as I have just learned. Also, in addition to being an LCSW, I have a Doctorate degree in Education, dealing with underperforming students between the ages of 5 and 10”.

“LCSW”, Benji asked. “Can you tell the court what that stands for?”

“Yes”, Dorothy continued. “It stands for Licensed Clinical Social Worker. Most of my work has been with children, specifically with ones who have been remedially challenged, due to things like poverty or broken homes”.

"And have you just recently learned that you have some previous dealings with Ms. McCullen?"

"Well, yes I did, Mr. Solomon, but I didn't know about it until I arrived in court this morning."

"Based on your reviewing this case", Benji continued, "I understand that you have some opinions about what would be in the best interest for this child?"

"Well, actually, in addition to that report, I can also provide this court with some anecdotal information about Ms. McCullen, as well".

"Proceed", the judge said.

"As I previously stated, I conduct a reading program to children in various parks in the city. One such park is Galagher Park, which is where I met Barbara. At first, she was reticent to join the circle, usually an indication of under-socialization".

"Under-socialization?" Benji interjected.

"Yes", Dorothy continued. "A condition where children are raised by an indigent parent, typically a single parent".

"Do you mean an unmarried parent?" Benji interjected.

"Not necessarily. I mean one parent, typically the mother. Occasionally, when a mother is homeless, they will live on the streets and attempt to care for their children at the same time."

"*Attempt* to care for their children?" Benji chimed in again.

"Yes, Mr. Solomon. Being homeless, being indigent is mind-boggling for anyone, let alone being the mother of a child. There is virtually no way for a parent, a mother to face the daily grinds of being homeless with the responsibilities of bringing up a child.

"In matters such as nutrition and hygiene?" Benji continued.

"That is the least of their problems. Being able to nurture their children, support their children emotionally…*love* their children is practically impossible. It places the child into a very deep hole. Often times, the parents are afraid to turn to social agencies, for fear they will lose custody of their child."

Benji took off his glasses and picked up a report off of the table. "Let's get back to Barbara and your experiences with her in the park."

"Okay", Dorothy continued. "When I asked Barbara her name, she was reluctant to tell me what it was. This indicates a lack of self-awareness and a feeling of shame and fear involving herself in self-disclosure that may result in further ridicule or strive."

"What did she do instead?" Benji cleaned his glasses waiting for Dorothy's answer.

"She told me…she had no name. I mistakenly heard her to say that her name was Nola. A child with a well-adjusted self-image would have corrected me and told me what they name was. Barbara was so lacking in those skills that not only did she let me call her Nola, she let all of the other kids call her that, too".

"Did she make friends with the other children?" Benji questioned.

"Well, she did but she was very awkward around the other children. She asked them questions about their own socialization', Dorothy answered.

"What did that indicate to you?" Benji asked.

"Objection, your Honor!" Whitcomb was on his feet. "Mr. Raetzke can't know what was in someone else's mind".

Looking at Whitcomb with a disgusted look, Benji said "I will rephrase. What *if anything* did that indicate to you?"

"It indicated that she was severely lacking in social skills. Many of the things that the other children took for granted were matters of deep mystery to her", Dorothy said.

"How severe do you feel this situation was?" Benji went on.

"About as severe as I have ever seen it". Dorothy went on. "I was in the midst of filing a formal report with Child and Family Services and having the child picked up. This is a copy of a report I filled with Officer Robert Sullivan. I had instructed him to detain her and her mother for questioning…and then, they just stopped coming to the park".

"Did you put forth any efforts to locate her?" Benji asked.

"Yes, but with as little information as I had, it wasn't easy. I had police officers maintain a visual search, plus I entered the name 'Nola' into the database".

"Based on your findings in this case, are you able to formulate an opinion about what is best for Ms. McCullen?"

"Yes, I do, Mr. Solomon. As I see it, there are three options, here. Barbara can be sent to foster care, she can be sent to live with her mother or she can be sent back to her father. In my opinion, foster care, really is out of the question. The only time children are sent to foster care is when there is no functional parental structure in place where the child can be nurtured."

Benji leaned forward. “Of the remaining two, which do you see as being in the best interest if the child”.

Dorothy looked at Benji like his question was ridiculous. “Sir, the choice is simple. Send this child home…with her father!” At that, my side of the table exploded with clapping and hollering.

“Thank you, Ms….ah Dr. Raetzke”, Benji concluded.

“Please keep in mind that Dr. Raetzke’s testimony is only to provide a broad brush into the case and her testimony is not meant to be admitted as evidence”, the judge said.

“Excuse me, your Honor”, Benji stood up. “Dr. Raetzke had a relationship, despite how short or nonchalant it may have been with my client. Certainly, that should be considered into your findings.”

“Yes, Mr. Solomon”, the judge continued, “Dr. Raetke’s direct contact with Barbara can be considered as evidence, but *only* her direct dealings with her. Any other testimony should be considered theoretical”. He gathered up some paperwork, put on his glasses, banged his gavel on the table and said, “This court will stand in recess, awaiting my ruling for one hour”.

I turned to Benji and said “That seemed like a good thing”.

Benji looked back and said “Well, it wasn’t a bad thing. Let’s see what that judge can cook up for us now”. At that, the courtroom got very still. I felt a little hand take mine.

We chose to wait in the courtroom during the judge’s deliberation. Buttercup and I colored out of a coloring book she kept in a backpack. Benji was on his cell phone frequently.

Eventually, the judge returned to the courtroom. There was a long silence. The judge wrote notes on what looked to be a legal pad on his desk. Finally, after several minutes, he was ready to address the court.

"This court", the judge began, "finds the sanctity of parenthood to be at the bedrock of our society. It is considered even more fundamental than that of marriage itself. The ties between a parent and a child can be stronger than the ties of a man and wife. Further, this court also finds that the institution of motherhood to be typically the strongest of them all. Even animals in the wild have demonstrated strong maternal instincts. Mothers of animals with much less intelligence than humans have been known to fight to their own deaths to protect their children.

Having stated all of that, Mr. Cullen…"

"McCullen, your Honor" I interrupted. I had my name legally re-changed to my real name: Daniel Patrick *Mc*Cullen". The 'Crime of the Century' paperwork that I have given Benji last week was the forms that would return my name back to my real name. Benji, somehow, got through all of the legal wranglings and had them processed much quicker than I ever would have.

"I see" the judge continued. "Mr. *Mc*Cullen brings up an excellent point. Fathers, of course can love their children as much or more than the child's mother.

This court has been asked to rule on a weighty decision: whether it should abide with the time-honored tradition of reuniting children with their mothers or to dismiss years, possible hundreds of years of tradition and ignore those customs.

In considering this case, I see no reason to potentially fix that, which is not broken. Ms. Novak and her experts have very eloquently argued why Barbara should be returned to Ms. Novak. Reasons such as 'Ms. Novak's sense of person would be returned to her through the care and nurturing of her daughter' have been introduced. Those are sound reasons to return Barbara to the care of her mother – as far as Ms. Novak is concerned. It doesn't take into consideration what would be fair and just for Barbara.

It is clear to see that Mr. McCullen and his daughter, Barbara have a nurturing relationship. He not only told this court how much he loves her, but has demonstrated it repeatedly throughout the weeks we have seen the two of them in court together. What is more important to this court and to me is that she deeply loves him, as well.

As I previously stated, I see no reason to fix something that is not broken. It is in doing so, Mr. McCullen, that I have no intention of ordering Barbara – 'Buttercup' to report to a foster home. Further, I have no intention of seeing your motion carried out. I am so ordering that Mr. Solomon's motion to place Barbara D. McCullen in the care of Gloria Jean Novak to be vacated, and I further order that custody of Ms. Barbara D. Mc Cullen shall be granted to her father, Daniel McCullen. This court stands adjourned".

I leaned over to Benji. "What just happened?" I asked.

"You just saw justice being served", Benji answered with a wink.

I looked over at Buttercup who looked confused.

"Honey, did you hear that?" I asked.

"Yes", she responded, "What does it mean? Why is everybody so happy? Why does Gloria Jean look so mad?"

""*Because*, the judge said you can come *home* and live with *me*", I exclaimed.

"Forever?" she asked.

"Forever and ever" I hollered, "Till Hell bubbles over".

A shocked smile shot across Buttercup's face as she put her hand over her mouth "Ahh! You said a 'swear'"! She giggled.

"Yes and in COURT, no less!" I grabbed her under her arms and swung her around in circles.

Whitcomb was on his feet.

"Your Honor, the People object. We have not presented our entire case yet", Whitcomb continued.

"You have as far as I am concerned", the judge continued.

"Your Honor…" Whitcomb broke in.

"Mr. Whitcomb, the People can refile at a later date if they want", the judge said.

"Your Honor, you can count on it", Whitcomb exclaimed.

"You do what you need to do, Mr. Whitcomb", the judge continued, "but for now, this court has ruled". The judge stood up and walked out of the court.

Toodles, who was sitting three rows behind us, was jumping up and down. She ran over to Buttercup and I and began to hug both of us. Soon all three of us were jumping up and down. Toodles released me and went over and hugged Benji. I put Buttercup on the floor and took her hand.

"Let's GO **HOME**, Buttercup", I said, walking toward the door.

Buttercup stopped and walked back to the prosecution table. She stopped in front of Charles Whitcomb. She took the flowered scarf off of Murgatroid's neck and placed it on the table next to Whitcomb, who was packing papers into briefcases and boxes.

"Here, Mr. Whitcomb", Buttercup said. "You look like you could use a friend", she said, as she walked back to me.

"Buttercup!" I explained with a shock, "You just gave Murgatroid away!" I picked her up and cradled her in my arms. She took the flowered scarf and stuck in the breast pocket of my shirt.

"I don't need him anymore. I got you now", she said and smiled, as she threw her arms around my neck. Toodles and Benji both laughed.

Chapter 27
"Buttercup's Musings"

I had this feeling that things would turn out okay. I will start first grade soon. Some kids are nervous about going to school, but after what I have been through, I don't think I would be nervous if wild animals sat in the desk next to mine. After all, my dad liked to make promises to me and he was big on making me make promises back to him. He made sure I never broke any of my promises and he certainly never broke any of his promises to me.

I still have a big bedroom and toys and clothes all over the place, but I would give them all back in a second. Someone could take all that away and give me my dirty blue jumper back and I would be happy as long as my dad was there with me. That is all I need – that is all I ever needed; cross my heart!

Chapter 28
"Gloria Jean's Remembering"

I really didn't care one way or the other if I got Buttercup back or not. In fact, if I did get her back, it may have been worse, for me and for her, but especially me. It probably would have just meant more work for me. If I learned anything about myself, it is that sober or high, I am pretty selfish. Having one more person to take care of was one person more than I preferred.

If I did get her back, I would probably screw it up anyway. After all, I did a pretty good job of screwing it up in the first place. However, looking back at it, I am amazed that I was able to hold it all together for as long as I did.

Well, I am young. If this "mommy" thing ever strikes me again, I guess I can always find some guy somewhere to help me pound out another one – although that one was awfully cute. Maybe the next one will be even cuter.

Chapter 29
"Danny Reflects"

Six years ago, I worked in a little record store, selling vintage records and thought I was happy. Five years ago, I sold my soul to the devil and became really unhappy. Three months ago, I got cold water splashed in my face, and learned what happiness was. I thought happiness would come with money. I was wrong. I thought happiness would come through prestige. I was really wrong.

Maybe I had to be really unhappy so that when happiness came around, I would recognize it. Maybe I had to work all of those hours and make all of that money as a part of a plan. After all, if I wasn't wealthy, I never would have been able to hire Benji Solomon and Gloria Jean would have ended up taking Buttercup away from me. And where would that have left me? Simple: all alone!

So, it took Buttercup to teach me what happiness was. She didn't stop with me, either. She taught everyone else at Gifford, Larkin and Glen the same lesson. She brought her bright, contagious smile into their lives and everyone seemed to simultaneously grow hearts. If you can get cold-hearted investment bankers to grow hearts, you can make tulips sprout in the middle of the desert.

I took the money from the severance package and purchased Scarlatti's Vintage Record Store. Scarlatti didn't know me directly, but he knew of me, from my previous record selling life. He was happy that a true connoisseur of vintage music would take over the company and gladly agreed to work in the store for the first six months to assure a smooth turn-over.

Since the investment firm didn't need me, they didn't need Toodles, either - But Scarlatti's did. Someone had to manage the books, order merchandise and handle the Internet orders, something Scarlatti never even thought of. Ms. Johnson's daycare center has a bus that will drop Buttercup off at the door every day at 4:00. There is a room in the back that we can fill with toys that she can play in until the store closes at 6:00.

Scarlatti made one point very clear: after he was out of the picture, we would have to change the name of the store. Buttercup and Toodles and I talked about it and we all agreed. We decided that it had to be something distinctive, yet catchy. It should be simple, yet hold sentimental value for us. On February 1st we rededicated "Murgatroid's Vintage Records".

(46,765 words)

www.ingramcontent.com/pod-product-compliance
Lightning Source LLC
LaVergne TN
LVHW091324150826
845673LV00006B/1764

* 9 7 9 8 6 5 2 8 8 8 9 8 5 *